A HUSBAND

BY

CHRISTMAS

Lisa Ann Verge

Also by Lisa Ann Verge

King's Girls Series
HEAVEN IN HIS ARMS
THE WINTER HUSBAND

The Celtic Legends Series
TWICE UPON A TIME: Book One
THE FAERY BRIDE: Book Two
WILD HIGHLAND MAGIC: Book Three
THE CELTIC LEGENDS SERIES: BOX SET
THE O'MADDEN: A Novella

Stand Alone Historical Romance
HER PIRATE HEART
SING ME HOME
THE CAPTIVE KNIGHT
ROMANTIC JOURNEYS COLLECTION: BOX SET

Writing as Lisa Verge Higgins

THE PROPER CARE AND MAINTENANCE OF
FRIENDSHIP
ONE GOOD FRIEND DESERVES ANOTHER
FRIENDSHIP MAKES THE HEART GROW
FONDER
RANDOM ACTS OF KINDNESS
SENSELESS ACTS OF BEAUTY

About A Husband By Christmas
and the King's Girls Series

The stories in the King's Girls Series are inspired by real events. For those interested, here's the history behind the novels.

In 1663, the tiny, just-burgeoning colony of Quebec was dominated by rowdy young men in search of exploration and adventure, much to the chagrin of their French King, who had big ambitions.

To settle his far-roaming countrymen, King Louis XIV chose young women from orphanages and the French countryside, girls he honored by calling them his daughters. He gifted them dowries appropriate to frontier life and then shipped them off to present-day Canada to be married.

Eight hundred women sailed to a challenging future between 1663 and 1673. Known as *Filles du Roi*, they are now the honored maternal ancestors of a large portion of modern-day, French-speaking Quebecois.

Their stories are true—mine are fiction, inspired by their courage, boldness, and spirit.

Publishing History

Print edition published by Bay Street Press
Copyright © 2022 Lisa Ann Verge
Cover design by The Killion Group

CHAPTER ONE

The Settlement of Quebec, 1663

Such a swarm of handsome, eligible men.

Marietta, made dizzy by all the muscular activity around her, was grateful she sat, not stood, in the bluish shade cast by a snow-laden fir tree. The thick woolen blanket she sat upon couldn't quite stave off the chill from the frozen ground, though. With her gloved hands busy in her lap, she crafted long, resin-fragrant garlands as decorations for Christmas while keeping a sharp eye on the bachelors. She'd tasked them to clip short sprigs of fir, and they'd been happy to accommodate her wishes and those of her three female companions. Amid all too many grins and winks and banter, the gentlemen had thrown themselves into the task with more gusto than necessary, flirting madly as they tossed the fragrant, ice-speckled ends in a growing pile.

"Gentlemen," she said, raising her voice as if she were addressing unruly children, "I believe you've cut enough fir sprigs for us. Now would you be so kind as to fetch us some cuttings of that feathery white pine over there, the one with the long, softer needles?"

Casting glances toward the other tree, a good distance away, the men didn't look keen to comply, but Marietta didn't allow her smile to waver. As much as she enjoyed their lively company—and so did her friends, judging by the way the younger girls sitting around her giggled and flushed a pink attributable to much more than the Quebec chill—she herself could use a respite from the whirlwind activity and ceaseless flattery of the men. Ever since September, when she and these girls—as well as nearly a dozen other women not currently present—had arrived by ship to these shores, they had all been the singular object of unwavering attention from the settlement men. Very few Frenchwomen lived in this small, rough place, and so hordes of bachelors frequently came to gawk…and to court. She and the other unmarried women were the very first batch of what the government was calling King's Daughters, though they preferred to call themselves King's *Girls*, sent to this wilderness for the express purpose of marriage.

Nearly a dozen of her fellow King's Girls had married already. Only the four of them here remained.

Marietta had decided long ago, that in terms of weddings, hers would be the *last*.

"Come now, sirs." She stroked the prickly bough on her lap, and then gestured to the half-finished bough on the lap of the woman beside her. All of them had been working steadily since they'd marched through the snowy field to the edge of these impenetrable woods, but there was still much to do. "The cold is beginning to bite, and these Christmas boughs must be ready by tomorrow at midnight."

"Very well." The man who conceded was the eldest among the bunch, and thus the wisest, Marietta supposed. "Come on, men," he urged. "The last to reach that pine will be the last to return as well."

And then the men were off, racing one another, which birthed a fresh surge of giggles from the girls. Marietta frowned at the men's retreating backs, and then at the gigglers around her. She hadn't planned for such high spirits today. It had been Marietta's own idea to usher the remaining girls out of Madame Bourdon's stiflingly hot kitchen this morning, for it was crowded with cooks, and Madame Bourdon, her gentle host, seemed at her wit's end getting ready for the Christmas festivities. But Marietta hadn't anticipated the crowd of suitors hovering outside the house. She'd assumed the biting December cold would prevent them from gathering, but the men of Quebec were hardened to the freezing weather. And so what was supposed to be a quick trip to the nearby woods to collect some greenery had transformed into a courtship party, complete with brawny men wielding knives with dangerous inattention, risking their own fingers as they cut sprigs, much more intent on flirting and flattery than finesse.

Such a strange situation she'd put herself in when, back in Paris, she'd thrown in her lot with the King's Girls.

Fumbling in her borrowed fishermen's gloves, Marietta wound some twine tight around a bundle of stems, casting occasional glances toward the far pine. The manly crowd turned out to be the usual motley group of bachelors, whittled down over the last few months as the unmarried men of Quebec and the maidens from France paired off. She recognized a few government clerks, who, lacking knives, acted as porters, risking the sap that would ruin their coats and vests for a chance to take part in the merry event, even in so menial a way as carrying sprigs. She'd come to know one of the older men, who owned a warehouse in the lower town, where he made a good living storing trade goods and furs in anticipation of the spring ships. She was also familiar with a few tradesmen, a cooper, and a flushed-faced tavern keeper. There was only one man among this group whose acquaintance she hadn't yet made. A silent, rough-looking woodsman in fringed deerskin breeches, who stood out to her only because she knew most of his footloose kind had disappeared into the wilderness long before the onset of winter.

She looked away from him. She'd been in this settlement for only a few months, but it was long enough to learn that woods runners were a dangerously unreliable breed of man.

She would keep *that* bachelor away from the girls.

"Emilie." Marietta turned her head toward the girl sitting behind her as she pulled another handful of snipped branches onto her aproned lap. "Your cooper just might break his neck, the way he keeps twisting his head to check on you. Does he think another suitor will scoop you up if he fails to keep you in his line of sight?"

"He's not looking at *me*." Emilie was as

shy as a sparrow, a quality that Marietta suspected too many doltish men-in-a-hurry interpreted as disinterest, which was likely why the dainty creature was still unwed. "We're all sitting together, Marietta. Theo is just looking in our general direction—"

"Theo?" Marietta grinned, turning her attention back to her work. "So it's Theo now between you two?"

"I wager, Emilie," Delphine interjected, as the worst gossip of them all, all shining blue eyes and trembling blonde curls, "you'll get a proposal from him on Christmas."

"I... I..."

Marietta didn't need to turn back around to know Emilie was flushing a deeper shade of pink.

"Then we'll have a wedding for the New Year!" Delphine clapped her gloved hands and then folded her fingers. "Maybe two weddings, if my clerk ever summons the courage—"

"Don't let a single worry furrow your brow, Delphine." Marietta jerked her chin toward the clerk now making his way back to their blanket, his arms filled with white pine sprigs. "There'll be plenty of rum to go around tomorrow night at Madame Bourdon's after-midnight feast. That will surely loosen your clerk's tongue."

Isabelle piped up, mousy little Isabelle, always last, in her ever-breathless voice. "But what of you, Marietta?"

"Never mind me."

"But you need to marry too."

"I will marry, by and by." *When all you girls are settled and I have no one left to care for but myself.*

"But they all adore you," Isabelle persisted. "Every man down to the last."

Marietta frowned into her fur scarf and wondered if Isabelle was even conscious of the longing that suffused the poor girl's voice.

"You, Marietta," Isabelle persisted, "could have your pick of any one of those men—"

"Stop flattering me, Isabelle, you know how I despise that."

Isabelle shrugged. "You do get a lot of flattery."

Marietta lifted the heavy end of the bough across her lap so she could shift it down to more easily get access to the bare end. "And what good are such frivolous words spoken in the hope of provoking vanity? Never let a man turn your head with compliments on one's looks or figure or bearing, girls."

"Perhaps someday, I'll have that chance," Isabelle said, barking a little laugh. "To have my head turned too."

"Isabelle." Marietta put some iron into her voice. "Remember: attraction alone does not a strong marriage make."

Marietta gave the girl an eye, mentally willing her to believe the truth, even if the hurried courtships of Quebec seemed to put that adage to the test. Isabelle was a sweet girl, not unattractive, only a mite too thin, with dark shadows around her eyes that gave her a sickly look when seen in the wrong kind of light. Marietta conceded that it wasn't unnatural for men who lived in this wilderness, who understood how difficult life could be here, to be drawn to the sturdiest and the hardiest of women, those who glowed with health. If those men would but take a mere *moment* to get to know Isabelle better and experience her sweetness and generosity, how she anticipated everyone's needs and brought the best out in all the girls…then they would know what a boon Isabelle would be to any man as a wife.

Furthermore, beauty was fleeting and much overrated. What really mattered between a man and a woman, Marietta believed, were the commonalities of temperament and goals, and a mutual determination to settle down and build a family. *All* these girls needed to consider those qualities, and the men should as well, if they had any sense. Teaching these women how to navigate their choices among bachelors had been her determination ever since the violently rolling ship voyage from Dieppe to this settlement, when Marietta had found herself below decks with a bunch of shivering, wailing, regretful soon-to-be brides. As the eldest at twenty-four years of age and the only one who'd ever lived independently, she felt compelled to console and encourage them, stepping into the role of mother, mentor, matchmaker, and guide. She'd never told the girls so—for girls as young as these were likely to *rebel* against mothering—so she let herself be considered an older, wiser sister among them. Once in Quebec, it became clear that taking care of them meant keeping potential suitors for herself at bay, at least for a while. It had turned out to be a more difficult task than she had anticipated—the men were persistent and appeared to love the chase. But she was resolved. She would *not* choose a husband for herself until she shepherded her vulnerable, naive charges into happy unions. An effort that also gave her the proper amount of time to think about who'd be the best choice for herself.

"Now, Isabelle, we've spoken of this," Delphine ventured, breaking into Marietta's musing. "It is well known that our Marietta is seeking a certain kind of man."

"Yes," Isabelle breathed. "One who is clever enough to solve her riddle."

"Precisely." Marietta nodded. "The riddle I have put forth to the bachelors of Quebec is a test, as you know." That riddle worked for her twofold: it filtered her own marriage prospects, and it also kept the men confused, at bay, and more likely to turn away from her and focus attention on the other unmarried women, more eager to be wed…at least in theory. "Remember, you should be testing your suitors to make sure they will satisfy your expectations for your future. I very much hope each of you has composed a test of your own."

"You don't expect me to make up a riddle, do you?" Delphine blew a strand of pale hair off her brow. "I could *never*. I have no mind for that sort of thing."

"Not a riddle, a *test*. Of any kind. It could even be a series of questions. Of course, you don't have to use the same method as mine," Marietta added. "Find another way to reveal the quality you want to see in a husband. For me, I'm looking for wit and intelligence. Only a man with a brilliant mind can solve my riddle."

"Did I hear you mention the riddle, Mademoiselle Marietta?"

A shadow fell over her as she glanced up. The first of the men had returned, a clerk who tumbled his armful of pine clippings into the pile beside the blanket.

"She did," Delphine responded, in the more highly pitched voice she used around men she was interested in. "But you'll break my heart if you strive to court Marietta by solving her riddle—"

"I would never, Mademoiselle Delphine, for my eye is on another, but," added the clerk, casting a glance over his shoulder at the other men, approaching at their leisure, "I can tell you there are some who would pay a fortune in pelts to know the answer."

"Pay?" Marietta raised her head so quickly that her fur hat tumbled off her head and fell to the blanket behind her. "That is not in the spirit of the challenge, gentlemen!" She raised her voice to reach the men trailing the others, including that rough-looking stranger in the back. "I would never grant the opportunity to court me to a suitor who came to the riddle's solution in such a devious way."

"Have pity, woman." The warehouse owner swaggered closer, looking bearish in his luxurious coat, now speared with hundreds of spiky green needles. "For months, the men of Quebec have been laboring over that riddle. Everyone begins to suspect there is no answer to it at all."

"Nonsense." Marietta paused tying another bunch of twigs to the bough long enough to wag her gloved finger. "There *is* an answer, sir. For a man wise enough to perceive it."

"Twenty lines, it has. *Twenty.*" The warehouse owner threw up his hands. "Who can remember such a long riddle? And what if there's no man in all the settlement who can break such a puzzle, miss?"

"I refuse to believe that." Marietta pulled the thin hemp rope tight. "All you gentlemen are clever. Someone will eventually realize how simple it is."

Maybe, or maybe not. She was beginning to think that the riddle game she and her father had always played, making up word puzzles in the evenings in an effort to entertain and stump one another, was a rare expression of wit and perception that existed only between them.

She winced, waiting for the knife-sharp pang of grief to lessen. How she missed him, her laughing, affectionate, storytelling father. Perhaps she could have chosen a less memory-challenging test than a long riddle, but the word puzzle served her purpose well, and it granted her power. It was a rare and wonderful thing to be in control of who would court her, whom she would wed.

Were her father still alive today, they would be living outside Paris, and he would likely be arranging some socially spectacular union for her before she got too much older. A union between her and one of his most important diplomatic contacts, most likely. She'd been raised a diplomat's daughter, she understood the rules and expectations of her position, and she'd trusted her father not to *force* her into a marriage with someone she was unwilling to make a life with, for whatever reason.

But Papa had gone to heaven ahead of his time, only a few years after her mother. She'd been left without family, nearly penniless, having no country she could truly call her own. The lure of a mysterious new continent and the promise of a substantial dowry had convinced her to offer herself up to King Louis's new program to ship women to the settlements to marry…whomever.

But the riddle gave her an element of control over her future. She would not give up that power. At least not before the spring came, when a new group of King's Girls would undoubtedly arrive, and her current advantage would be diluted.

"Come, mademoiselle." The warehouse owner demanded her full attention by crouching down and offering a drooping sprig of needles. "Christmas Eve is tomorrow. Will you not be kind, in honor of the season, to grant all us poor suffering creatures a boon of some sort?"

"How shameless you are." She was tempted, for he'd spoken well. "Look at you, begging like that."

"'Tis the season of miracles." He shrugged, his smile splitting his reddish beard with a slash of straight, white teeth.

She narrowed her eyes at him. He was an

amusing man, this warehouse owner, and a rich one too. A woman could do much worse for a husband.

"If I may be so bold," he persisted, "and propose an idea. But first, tell me, Mademoiselle Marietta, have you decided who will sit next to you at Madame Bourdon's réveillon feast tomorrow night?"

"Madame Bourdon's oldest son," Marietta responded. "A twelve-year-old sitting at a table of adult guests for the first time is in need of serious monitoring."

"But certainly there will be a seat on *either* side of you. Who is to take the chair on your other side?"

Marietta frowned. She'd already assigned seats for her fellow unmarried King's Girls, making sure they were placed between the most prominent local bachelors, but she hadn't given her own seat a single thought beyond helping Madame Bourdon by promising to keep an eye on her rascally eldest son.

The warehouse owner's face brightened. She could tell he sensed a weakness as he leaned in. "Mademoiselle, you've led us all on a merry chase these past months. You're the most elusive doe of all. Of course, we all covet the prize of spending an evening by your side. Would you have us come to blows at the réveillon, fighting over who will sit in the chair next to yours for the midnight Christmas feast?"

She tsked. "Of course not."

"Then I propose a better way." The warehouse owner eyed the men standing on either side of him. "Make one of us earn that seat. Offer another riddle to us."

His words landed, and the men around him shouted their *yeas* like politicians at a wilderness parliament.

Marietta frowned as the tumult ebbed. "You'll all want an easier riddle, I suppose."

"To that," the warehouse owner exclaimed, "I won't object."

"I will not take back the first riddle," she warned, sensing she was being outmaneuvered. "Even if I choose to offer a second riddle, I will not take back the first. The second riddle wouldn't be an invitation for a courtship, only for a single evening by my side."

"Offer up a new riddle, then," one of the other clerks barked from the back of the crowd. "We've no objection to earning the honor, *belle petite*."

Marietta resisted the urge to roll her eyes. She didn't consider herself a pretty young thing, not in the way she believed the man meant it, as in she was a gentle and compliant creature like Isabelle. None of these men had bothered to get to know her well enough to learn that she'd been a motherless child for so long that she was fiercely independent, strict and inflexible in her resolve, or that she could wield a knife better than any of these men could imagine—in or out of the kitchen. That was the singular problem she perceived with this marry-off-the-bachelors-of-Quebec program of the king's. None of the couples had a chance to know each other long enough to see beneath superficial qualities.

With those thoughts in mind, she frowned at the gentlemen before her, breathing clouds of moisture into the chill air. Some stood, some crouched. The sun, so low on the horizon, speared hazy white light between their limbs. They all looked terribly desperate and yet hopeful, hanging on her next words.

"Oh, very well, gentlemen."

Shouts of triumph rose up, pierced by giddy squeals from the girls.

"*One* riddle," she reminded them. She yanked off one of the heavy fisherman's gloves borrowed from Monsieur Bourdon. It remained stuck by pine sap to the palm of her other gloved hand, as she raised a bare finger. "*One* evening."

They bobbed their heads and then slapped their hands on the shoulders of the crouching men, as if to hold them down. Collectively, they leaned close to listen. Not that this edge of the woods was noisy, for it wasn't. Any noise that came from the wooden houses and stone churches of the upper town had dimmed long before reaching them, on the far side of the open, snowy field.

She sighed into the expectant silence, glanced back at the girls around and behind her, her gaze lingering on Isabelle, whose wide, reddened eyes blinked, her face half swallowed by a fur muffler.

Turning back to the men, she said, "Listen closely, gentlemen. Here's my riddle:

I wound the heart and please the eye,
tell me what I am, by and by?"

In the chill air, the riddle hung. She watched each face as the men mentally worked through the possibilities. She couldn't help feeling a little thrill as the moment stretched. How she'd loved when she'd spoken a newly composed riddle to her father, and he, clutching the bowl of his pipe, would by inches lean deeper in the worn, overstuffed chair by the hearth and stare at the shadowed rafters until he inevitably worked out a solution.

Which he always did, she remembered with a fresh, sharp pang.

But no chance of that here, she realized, as the angle of the white stream of sun shifted with the passing of minutes. It was not a particularly challenging riddle, but it did require some flexibility of mind. She decided to give them plenty of time, so she slipped the fisherman's glove over her chill-pinkened hand and turned her attention to finishing the garland upon her lap, winding the twine so tightly that she snapped one of the stems of the clippings, releasing a fresh burst of the wood's resinous perfume.

"Come now, gentlemen," she murmured, as she finished weaving the bough and still no man answered. "Shall I give you a hint?"

They leaned in closer, heads bobbing.

"The answer is something not earned, easily lost, and of no value whatsoever," she added, squinting beyond their heads to the sky, which had turned a deeper shade of blue. "And yet it's too often praised to the skies."

"Mademoiselle," the warehouse owner chided. "You're making this all so difficult—"

"Beauty."

She started and turned toward the voice. When she saw who it was, her heart sank. The rough-looking stranger, that deerskin-clad woods runner, stood separate from the group, leaning against the trunk of the fir tree.

Could she have been mistaken that the answer had come from him? She raised her voice, though it strained her throat. "Please repeat your answer, sir."

"Beauty," he repeated, sliding a thumb under the sagging leather of his beaded belt. "Beauty pierces the heart and pleases the eye, and is too often considered a virtue and praised to the skies."

A great groan rose up among the men, as they straightened from their crouches and threw their arms in the air. She frowned at the winner and considered explaining the riddle further, which was usually necessary, but this stranger had already offered an explanation with terseness and clarity.

She took a good look at the man, his tousled, shoulder-length, dark-blond hair and especially the furrowed scar that ran down his cheek from brow to jaw, a scar that spoke of sharp knives and thrown tomahawks. She would have been happier if the riddle had been solved by any other man in the crowd. To think, she'd committed herself to an evening with such company, a man whose clothing and attitude personified unfettered freedom, restlessness, a hunger for adventure, an aversion to responsibility. She'd been told from the moment she and the other King's Girls had stepped on shore that men such as these woods runners made up the majority of the bachelors of the settlement. Both Madame Bourdon and Marie de l'Incarnation, the mother superior of the Ursuline nuns—two of the most senior female inhabitants of the young settlement—had warned the King's Girls to be careful when considering the woods runners as husbands. Over the past months, Marietta had come to understand and confirm these esteemed ladies' opinions. Wilderness wanderers like this man represented everything Marietta *didn't* want in a wedding partner.

Or even a dinner partner.

And yet…this woods runner had solved the riddle.

"Well done, sir." She *would* hold to her word, no matter what. Such things defined a woman's—and a man's—character. "You have won the challenge, thus you may sit by my side at the réveillon."

"I look forward to the evening."

She could not say the same, but it was only one evening. It wouldn't be the first she'd spent in the presence of a less than perfect match. She braced herself as he pushed away from the tree trunk with one shoulder, strode to her in two quick strides, and bent to sweep up the heavy, now-finished bough from her lap. "I shall carry this back to Madame Bourdon's with you, mademoiselle," he said in a surprisingly cultured voice, "so we may become better acquainted before tomorrow's dinner."

CHAPTER TWO

Her eyes, thickly fringed with lashes, screamed *you're being presumptuous,* but Philippe made an effort to dim her outrage with the friendliest smile he could manage. In his experience, smiles usually worked to bring around even the most reticent of Frenchwomen, but when he held out his hand to help her up from her seat on the blanket, the enticing woman called Marietta didn't take it with gratitude. Instead, she narrowed those lovely eyes and went still with suspicion, like a dark-eyed doe hearing a crack of a twig in the woods.

Good instincts, this woman. For his intent was not completely proper. His thoughts were running away from him, prodded, as she tilted her chin up from her fur muffler, by the sight of rosy lips. They were soft and in the shape of a pout, as if begging for a kiss he craved with a ridiculous fierceness for no reason he could discern, other than that she was a striking woman, and he a man who usually held himself in better control.

In time, he would kiss those lips.

In time.

She placed a gloved hand in his in a way that suggested the act was not completely in accordance with her will. Her elk-skin fisherman's gloves were thickly lined, and he could barely feel the shape of her bones within. Shamelessly showing off, he pulled her to her feet—what a light woman. There couldn't be much of her beneath the bulky trappings of shawls and cloak. And yet, even with all the wrappings, she'd glowed in a way different from the other girls. He'd noticed it from the start. She was a queen surrounded by pale, faded attendants. Her black hair gleamed with reflected light, like the streak of stars against the velvet night.

Hell.

He hadn't come to the upper town of Quebec today to be charmed.

What was wrong with him?

"Perhaps we all should head back," the woman named Marietta murmured as she shook her apron free of needles and swept up her fallen fur hat. "The light is failing fast. Better to finish this task by the glow of a warm fire. Gentlemen, would you be so kind as to load the deer sleigh with the clippings that remain, while we ladies walk ahead?"

She dropped her hand from his grip, set her hat on her head, and took a careful step into the tracks of knee-deep snow, following the furrowed way flattened by the deer sled and boot prints made upon their earlier trek here. He didn't need to read her mind to sense she was fleeing his presence, but he followed, anyway, because…that was where his feet and inclinations led him. In some practical part of his mind, he wished he'd worn snowshoes, for in his opinion, it was foolish not to wear snowshoes when traveling across the deep drifts that covered this field.

Since it was not yet the moon of the crusted snow, when temperatures dipped well below freezing, and created a hard crust on the surface, snowshoes were the better choice. But she didn't have them on either, and when he'd chosen to join their lively party, he hadn't been thinking about snowdrifts or snowshoes. Only of the woman he'd glimpsed bounding out of a fine home into a crescent of male admirers.

A bolt of lightning couldn't have hit him with the same effect as that sight. Without a moment of hesitation, he'd ignored the plans he'd made for the afternoon and joined the crowd. He convinced himself it was just curiosity that led him to follow the high-spirited party across the field. For it was an odd thing these people were doing—weaving pine boughs. His adoptive Abenaki family wouldn't bother to spend so much time or energy to festoon the bark walls of their winter hunting huts in such a way. But such were the ways of settlement people, French like himself. He'd lived apart from their traditions for so long that sometimes, he forgot them.

But he hadn't forgotten the réveillon, the midnight feast everyone celebrated after Christmas midnight mass. Who could ever forget such feasting and music and dancing and laughter, especially a man who'd once been a half-starving boy on the streets of Dieppe? When Philippe had heard the warehouse owner mention that there was an empty seat beside this woman at the feast, Philippe had become determined to win an invitation, not only for the food and revelry and nostalgia, but mostly for the gift of an evening by this woman's side.

So he solved her riddle.

If only she would stop trying to outpace him, walking with her head down as if unaware of his presence beside her, or, more likely, just unwilling to engage in conversation.

"Mademoiselle," he said, offering his elbow to catch her attention. An Abenaki woman might take the offer of help in walking as an insult, but he remembered that most Frenchwomen would welcome such an offer as a courtesy. "There is ice beneath the snow. Please take my arm."

She ran her glove under his elbow and slid him a sideways glance that had him catching his breath. "Since it appears we are to be spending some time together, I shall introduce myself. My name is Marietta."

"I am…Philippe." He considered giving her the name his adoptive Abenaki family called him, but she might not be able to pronounce it, and everyone in the settlements called him by his French name, anyway. "Philippe Martineau."

"Philippe." She did something odd with the sound, playing with it with her tongue. He'd noticed that she had a slight, unusual accent that bounced up at the end of words, but he couldn't place it. "Why are you not roaming about in the winter wilderness with others of your kind?"

He asked, "My kind?"

"Woods runners, *voyageurs,* traders with the far western tribes?"

"Ah." Was he so easily perceived? He glanced over his shoulder and watched the other men pull the low-slung deer sleigh.

noticing for the first time their woolen French clothing, the lack of buckskin and leggings, the only nod to the bitter cold, fashionable fur hats and mufflers. He'd paid little mind to those men as he'd trailed behind the crowd earlier—distracted by the queen among them—but now he realized he was the only one fully dressed correctly for the country and season.

"Indeed, I had planned to be in the wild," he confessed. He sensed she would not like his answer, but he'd been raised to speak truth, always. Both of his fathers had taught him that wisdom. "But I and my business partner missed the season this year." Complication after complication had plagued his and his friend Andre's plans. With no obligations or responsibilities elsewhere, Philippe had promised to stay in the settlement with Andre over the winter to better prepare for the following fall. "We will be making an expedition to the west in the coming September."

"And how did you come to answer my riddle so quickly?"

He squinted into the dull sun just starting to sink into the far horizon. "The riddle was not hard." He shrugged. "I looked at your beauty, was pierced to the heart, and thus knew the answer."

She turned her face away, showing him only a chill-pinkened cheek. He felt as if the sun had dipped behind a mountaintop. Had he not spoken truth? She seemed to consider it flirtation. Which he supposed it was.

If she didn't like it, he had to find another way to intrigue her. "You are a King's Daughter, yes?"

"Of course."

"Why did you become one and come here?"

She stumbled, and he knew he'd surprised her, and that pleased him. Such a woman would be used to being worshiped, so would hold her affections tight, unless she was taken off guard.

"That's a personal question. You are quite blunt, sir," she said, setting her gaze straight forward, to the line of steep, wooden-shingled homes coming closer. "If you must know, I came to Quebec for the adventure, I suppose."

"I understand adventure." For him, the flap of canvas sails at the port of Dieppe had stirred him to cross the sea. "It is what brought many of us here, to the woods, the wild—"

"It's not quite the same, I assure you." She spoke as if she'd repeated the words a thousand times. "Back in France, before I joined the King's Girls, I had few choices. I'm a child of a Florentine mother and a French diplomat of a father—"

There, he thought, the accent.

"—who were always moving from country to country to country. When they died, I had no home to return to, no country I could truly call my own."

"Home," he murmured, "can be an elusive thing."

"Indeed." Her pretty brow rippled. "And so I leapt at the king's offer and now find myself here. That is why I am a King's Girl."

"I am sorry for the loss of your parents." His throat tightened. He'd lost his parents young too. "Life is a shadow that runs across the snow and loses itself in the sunset."

She paused, glancing up at him. "Is that a riddle?"

"No."

"Poetry, then?"

"I suppose." How her skin glowed in that upturned face. "It's something my…father once said."

"Was he a poet?"

"In a way." How his French father would laugh if he'd ever been called such a thing, in his bloody apron while he cut up fish and discarded the heads at the port of Dieppe. On the other hand, his Abenaki father would take such a compliment as a point of pride. He'd long discovered that the Abenaki language drew strongly from the land, and being able to express oneself around the council fires with flair was an honored quality.

She said, "Are you educated, sir?"

He turned his attention to where he set his boots in the snow, considering the question, knowing she threw it at him expecting an answer as frank as the one she'd given him. The truth was, he'd had many different kinds of education. As a boy living under the docks of Dieppe, learning to steal food and catch his own fish. And, for a brief time, educated under the tutelage of a friar, back when his family had a single season of prosperity. As a young man welcomed as a guest into a tribe of Abenaki, learning the skills of surviving a Quebec winter.

"Once, a long time ago," he said, choosing his words carefully, "a kindly priest taught me my letters and numbers."

"And yet with only that education, you solved a riddle none of your peers could puzzle out."

"They are good men, but they think too hard." *And don't trust their instincts.* He shrugged. "The solution came to me as a revelation. As if I were in a waking dream."

She buried her chin in her fur muffler and quickened her pace as the depth of the snow tapered off to the hard-packed footpath that led to the row of wooden houses.

"I have answered one of your riddles," he said, sensing their time was short. "But what is this other riddle the men were speaking of?"

He wasn't sure why he was asking this question. Knowing the other riddle and solving it could come to naught. He was deep into plans for a trip to the west, he'd be gone with Andre for months, years, he had no time for a wife, no intention of marrying anyone yet, and this Marietta was likely not the kind of woman interested in any more casual, or purely carnal, relationship. And yet he couldn't help asking. He felt like a buck in the waning warmth of September, compelled to follow the faintest scent of a doe, all urge and no sense.

"I choose *not* to tell you that riddle right now, Monsieur Martineau." She stopped before one of the houses, the house he'd seen her emerge from only hours ago, glass windows glowing with golden light in the darkening of the twilight. "I think that's for the best."

"Then what is the purpose of your riddle, Miss Marietta, if not to be shared and solved?"

"Those men know the riddle by heart," she said, lifting her rounded little chin toward the crowd of men and giggling women who had followed them, now pulling up the sleigh before this house of golden light. "You can always ask them."

"But I ask you."

"You are like a dog with a bone, sir." She frowned. "But if I were to tell you the original riddle and you discerned its secrets as quickly as you just did the last, I might find myself under more obligation than a single dinner by your side."

His insides lit up with warmth. "Ah, *kpipskwáhsawe*, is that so bad a fate?"

She blinked at the unfamiliar word, and only then did he realize he'd spoken Abenaki, calling her his flower of the woods.

Hell.

"I don't know, sir," she said, a little breathless. "I don't know who you are. I've hardly had time to know you."

"I'll tell you anything you want."

"But not now." She tossed her head toward the light pouring through the window.

"I have duties I must attend to."

He couldn't look away from her. There was something so compelling about this woman—he struggled to figure out what. She met his eye like an equal, and he sensed she had very high expectations of men's behavior around her, like any queen. This Marietta was a curious creature who held some strange power over him, a power he didn't understand and should probably avoid.

And yet, the words came. "Tomorrow night, then."

"Yes." She seized the bough across his shoulders and tugged it, stepping back to snake it off until it trailed in the packed snow. "At the midnight feast, I will repeat the riddle one last time for you…and for all."

CHAPTER THREE

After midnight, the church doors burst open to a biting chill.

Marietta, her arms linked with Delphine and Emilie, raised her face to the blue-white light of the moonlit sky while the freezing air nipped her nose. The one thing about this new world that continued to astonish her, compared to the cramped, narrow alleyways of Paris where she'd lived with her father, was the crystalline clarity of the air.

If she reached up, surely she could touch the stars.

"It's Christmas Day," Delphine blurted to no one in particular as their boots crunched over the snow. "I'm so hungry, I swear my stomach is in my heels."

Marietta laughed, and so did Emilie, their breath misting before them. The weeks leading up to Christmas were days of prayer, abstinence, and fasting, so everyone was ravenous. The crowd that poured from the church strode with great determination toward their warm hearths and homes, where the tables were likely already laid. Everyone had spent weeks preparing for the feast after midnight mass, the réveillon.

The night air quivered with excitement, it seemed to Marietta. Big changes were coming. As the leading lady of the upper town of Quebec, her hostess, Madame Bourdon, had chosen many of tonight's guests not just from the highest rankings of the local society, but also, with a mind toward her unmarried girls, from among the most eligible bachelors in the area, no matter their social status. For certain, there would be flirting and chatter and, in the days to come, perhaps the hope of several weddings. Marietta had prayed that Delphine's clerk would ask for Delphine's hand tonight, that Emilie's cooper might finally slide a ring on her finger, and that Isabelle's quiet loveliness, bathed in the gentle light of candles, might attract the romantic notice of a government administrator or well-off merchant smart enough to sense her worth, yet who didn't require a wife to embrace the duties of churning butter or butchering game or any other strenuous task.

As for herself…well. She'd embraced the responsibility of seeing her friends settled, so only when the last was promised in matrimony would she allow herself to turn her full attention to her own future. In that light, she realized that yesterday, it had been wisdom, not weakness, when she'd committed herself to an evening with a woods runner. Tonight was solely for her friends, and so her unlikely dinner partner would be the perfect bulwark against *other* entreaties for her favor. Of course, she intended to kindly discourage Monsieur Martineau's attentions. No matter how brawny and handsome he was, no matter how unsettling she considered his searching blue eyes or how sharp his natural intelligence, the one thing she knew for sure was that Philippe Martineau couldn't be her husband.

She would not marry a man already planning to abandon any future wife in favor of the wilderness.

After her father's death, she'd spent enough time alone.

The front door to Madame Bourdon's home flew open wide in welcome when Marietta, Delphine, and Emilie arrived. Madame Bourdon and Isabelle had left mass a few minutes early to make sure the beeswax candles were lit all around the dining room and the platters were already on the tables with all the necessary serving pewter. Marietta, Delphine, and Emilie stepped into the crush of merry, laughing visitors in the entranceway, kicking the ice from their boots, divesting themselves of fur cloaks and hats and mufflers and gloves. Under the direction of Madame Bourdon's many younger children, compelled into the duties of butlers and valets, they pitched in to help pile everything over the banister by the stairs to the upper level, twisted with the pine boughs they'd labored so hard to complete the day before. The warmth of the dining room made Marietta's numb cheeks tingle, the scent of the food made her stomach growl, and the light from the candles and the roaring fire cast the whole room in a flickering, golden glow.

Under the low rafters, the dining table was double the usual length because of the trestle table added to the far end to accommodate more than two dozen guests. As those guests flooded in, they checked the name cards on each setting, written in Madame Bourdon's flowing script, before each took his or her place. With so many guests of different social stature invited, Marietta admired her hostess's wisdom in seating the king's newly appointed governor of the colony beside the newly elected mayor of the settlement. Across from both sat the Jesuit bishop. These three most powerful men sat at places of honor at the table's head with Monsieur Bourdon presiding and Madame by his right hand. Yet within conversational distance, between Marietta and the head of the table, sat several other men, some dressed in velvets that marked them as gentlemen of means or elevated birth, others dressed in the Sunday best of well-off artisans and craftsmen and merchants, with Isabelle, Emelie, and Delphine staggered among them. The presence of the young women so close to the head of the table would ensure that the conversation wouldn't be completely monopolized by politics.

As Marietta took her own place on the far side of the salt and beside her hostess's eldest son, a twelve-year-old who needed supervision, she noticed that there were many more guests than seats at the table. Men of a certain status tended to bring their chief clerks or servants without notifying the hostess. Some of those unexpected guests bowed out and headed toward the less-formal atmosphere of the kitchens in the back of the house, while others perched themselves on chairs arranged against the walls on either side of the table, close enough to be a part of the conversation while being forced to balance dinner on their laps.

As Marietta straightened the folds of her

primrose-colored dress, she caught sight of two more guests stepping into the room. She didn't recognize the leader of the two, but she sat up straight in her chair as she glimpsed who followed. He was not hard to mistake, with that long scar that furrowed one cheek from temple all the way to a tuft of trimmed blond beard.

"Monsieur Martineau." Her wave caught his attention, as well as the beam of his direct gaze. She lowered her arm and patted the seat beside her. "I believe your place is here."

He gallantly swept off his hat, festooned with a feather, to reveal that he'd combed his shaggy dark blond hair off his brow. Trying to impress her, perhaps? He certainly did so when he tossed his expensive hat carelessly toward one of Madame Bourdon's younger sons, who caught it with a broad grin. After a wink at the child and a tap on the boy's cheek, Philippe made his way to her, his velvet coat with its long line of unfastened buttons splitting to show he still wore deerskin breeches and high, furred boots.

Who was this man? A Frenchman? A

Canadien, as many of the long-time settlers were called? A woods runner? Perhaps he was *trying* to intrigue her with his many contradictions.

Bishop Laval began the blessing as Philippe took his place beside her, his blue eyes dancing. She closed her eyes in piety, but that only made her more conscious of his scent, a billow of ice-crusted pinewoods and…what? Nutmeg? Cinnamon? Fresh-shaved wood? The spicy aroma brought to mind the wild creatures of her grandmother's fairy tales, magical beings from the deepest forests.

What fancy, what foolishness.

And she had not yet even taken a single quaff of holiday cheer.

As the bishop finished the blessing, the boards of the table groaned as platters were shifted, as Monsieur Bourdon exerted some force to carve the clove-studded ham, as the pitcher of fine wine made its way around the table and tin cups were filled with the elixir. Marietta couldn't decide what she would eat first. Should she choose a slice of a pigeon pie, or fresh-roasted venison tenderloin from a buck caught only yesterday? She was sorely tempted by the savory, buttery, double-crusted meat pie, a *tourtière* that Isabelle and Madame Bourdon had labored over for hours and now sat, steaming and fragrant, in a cast-iron pot in the middle of the table. There were hearty loaves of wheat-flour bread, thick slices of sweet raisin bread, vinegared root vegetables from the fall harvest, and glistening wild berry preserves from the summer kitchen. The bowls and platters were being passed around by the guests themselves, since there were few servants in Quebec, and those of the Bourdons were having a celebration in the kitchens or with their own families elsewhere.

"Merry Christmas, Marietta."

Philippe's voice rumbled low, at a pitch only she could hear in the churn of the conversation. Marietta took the tin cup of wine from Philippe's hand, catching his gaze above the rim. Funny how candlelight had a way of smudging the roughness from a man's face. Or maybe she was just infused with the generosity and spirit of the season. As she took a deep sip of the fine vintage, Marietta noticed that he had not only combed back his hair, but he'd also scrubbed his face since she'd last seen him. No longer did he appear so much the sun-bronzed outdoorsman whose broad brow had been speckled with bark and pine and the usual dirty labor of a woodsman. Now his cheeks were closely shaved and his short blond beard neatly trimmed. This Philippe Martineau who sat beside her could almost pass for a man of the upper town. A clerk or an administrator, a diplomat or a politician, a merchant of some means.

Except for that frank, hungry look in his eye.

"Merry Christmas to you too, Monsieur Martineau." She clanked her tin cup against his and determined to puzzle him out before the night was through. "I'm flattered that you were able to change your plans with such short notice to join us."

"I had no plans that needed change." His teeth flashed, which made his scar whiten, and she got the distinct impression that Philippe knew she was digging for information. "I have no blood ties in the settlement, mademoiselle. Nor a wife or children."

"No siblings, no parents?"

He paused. Something moved behind his eyes. "My parents in France died some time ago."

Sympathy shot through her, and she regretted asking the question. It had been nearly two years since she'd lost her darling Papa, longer since the loss of her mother, and yet any reminder still cut her to the bone. As it clearly did for Philippe. In the awkward pause that followed, the boy on her other side tapped her on the shoulder with the edge of a plate, as she discovered when she turned toward him. She took the platter of sliced ham out of his hands and presented it to Philippe. Philippe plunged the tip of his knife into one of the slices and slid it onto her plate before serving himself and then taking the plate and offering it farther down the table.

"I grew up in Dieppe," he said, turning back to her as if they hadn't had an awkward moment. "You may have been there yourself. I know many of the King's Daughters arrive here on ships that sailed from there."

"Indeed, I have been there." She remembered it as a large, loud town with many narrow winding streets and a port bristling with masts. A place of transition for those who didn't remain still for long. "The waterfront was such a busy place."

"My father worked at that port." Philippe reached for several slices of thick, hard-crusted bread, which he shared with her. "I knew when I was very young that one day, I would step upon one of those ships and sail to faraway places."

"From when you were young, you knew?" As free as the wind, the spirit of this man. She could almost feel the breeze coming off him. "I suppose that makes sense. You mentioned yesterday that you were planning a trip to go somewhere even more faraway, out west into the wilderness."

"Yes." Philippe tilted his head toward the good-looking youngish friend he'd arrived with, now sitting in one of the chairs against a wall. The ruddy young man balanced a plate on his lap as he leaned forward, starting a conversation with one of the administrators closer to the head of the table. "I arrived here with my business partner, Andre Lefebvre. He and I have great ambitions for the future."

"In the fur trade," she said, "I assume?"

"Of course."

Along with lumber, Marietta had learned that furs were the main export of the settlement, the lifeblood of its commerce. Every man at the table, even the bishop, had a hand in the industry. Ambition was an admirable thing if correctly channeled, but she couldn't figure out why Philippe's kind of ambition bothered her so.

"But also," Philippe added, tearing off a bite of bread, "we want to explore."

She raised her brows . "As in leave the settlements behind for an indefinite time?"

"That is the nature of exploration." His gaze wandered over her face. "You never know what you'll find."

She turned her attention to her plate, to cutting the ham and bringing it to her mouth, wondering why this new information—that his trip wouldn't even have a firm return date—should pinch her with disappointment. She shouldn't care. She'd already made up her mind. Philippe Martineau was not the kind of man she was looking for in a husband.

"It is a good thing, don't you think," he said, trying to draw her back into conversation, "to venture to new places, meet new people?"

She shrugged and took another sip of wine.

"Ah, come now, pretty Marietta," he teased. "You said yourself that you are a diplomat's daughter. You must understand what I'm talking about, having traveled widely."

"It's true." She swallowed a pang. "I've been all over Europe."

She pressed her lips together. It would be folly to admit to Philippe that every new place she and her family had moved to had felt like a glorious surprise. Nor could she admit that when, after her father's death, she'd heard about the king choosing girls to dower and ship across the sea, a part of her heart thrilled at the prospect of a new continent, a new culture, and a new adventure.

She'd put all that behind her.

It was a different experience to travel alone.

"Yes, I did enjoy traveling," she confessed. "But now I am ready to send roots deep into this lovely country."

"My roots go deep here too, but I can't help but wonder," he said. "It's such a grand, majestic place. How far west does the land stretch? And who are the peoples on it?"

Philippe glanced at the couple across the table from them, a young couple from one of the local tribes who were spending the winter close to the settlements. Leaning forward to be better heard, Philippe said something indecipherable to the young man—Ahano, a frequent guest at the Bourdons' table, along with his wife and two children. She didn't understand what the two men were saying to one another, but she recognized—with surprise and a jolt of rising respect—the cadence of the Abenaki language coming out of Philippe's mouth.

While they were talking, Marietta took the opportunity to turn toward Madame Bourdon's oldest son, reminding him to spread his linen on his lap, and to speak with the young clerk on *his* left once she turned back to converse with Philippe.

When she did turn back, she gently injected during a pause in their conversation, "I see you speak Abenaki, Monsieur Martineau."

"I *am* Abenaki." Philippe turned the full force of his dark blue eyes upon her. "The bear clan adopted me into their tribe years ago."

"Oh." She couldn't hide her puzzlement. She'd met many settlers who were of both French and native descent, and she knew plenty of Frenchmen who'd married into the various tribes, both for trading alliances and for pure affection, but this matter of "adoption" was a revelation to her.

And yet…it explained so much about this man, this bundle of contradictions, so much of him French, so much of him…not.

"Ahano and Niben were just telling me about their children," he said, nodding to the listening couple across the candlelight. "They have two young boys, and a third child on the way."

"I know about their boys"—favorite companions of Madame Bourdon's two younger sons—"but I had not heard that there was another child coming. Congratulations to you both."

"Ahano hopes it will be a girl this time," Philippe added. "Niben too, I suspect, but she will not say so aloud. I told them I hoped they would have a lovely baby girl with black hair and midnight-deep eyes."

He said this while staring pointedly at her dark hair, her dark eyes. Flattery always stiffened her spine, but the wine must be going to her head, because instead, a tingling passed through her body, leaving an unsettling languor in its wake.

Breathe, Marietta.

And put down the wine.

"How fanciful you are, sir. The child will be what the child will be, and a healthy child is the best we can pray for." She let her gaze shift to the iron pot in the middle of the table, just barely within reach of Philippe, and she chose to shift the conversation. "Would you be so kind as to ask your neighbor to share some of that tourtière in front of him?"

"My pleasure." He took her plate and made a request of his seated neighbor, who dug a serving spoon into the heavy bowl with hearty grace. As Philippe passed the plate back to her, Philippe's neighbor settled a portion of the tourtière upon Philippe's plate as well.

"*Magnifique,*" he said, after he took a bite. "Is it your creation, mademoiselle?"

"Not at all." She took a bite, enjoying for a moment the melting of the flaky crust. "I am capable of making a fine enough tourtière," she confessed, "but this level of craft is far above me. I chopped the meat and vegetables, but the one who put it all together and created this divine crust is the lovely young woman just over there, in conversation with the governor. "

Philippe's gaze flickered to Isabelle just as

the girl flashed an unexpectedly deep dimple. The candlelight bathed the girl in a golden glow. A sudden thought shot through Marietta's mind—perhaps Philippe would be a good match for Isabelle, for his lengthy absences from the settlement would leave Isabelle taxed with many fewer household duties—but along with the thought came a strange, odd resistance.

"As a man used to eating the flesh of moose and bear fresh from the kill," Philippe said, scooping up more tourtière, "I have great appreciation for such skills. Her husband is a lucky man."

"No husband, not yet," she said, thinking the match couldn't possibly work, though she struggled to come up with a solid reason why.

"Well, I'm sure her skills will soon be appreciated by some genteel bachelor with a refined palate."

But not me.

With those words ringing in her mind, she looked at Philippe directly. He hadn't said the words aloud, but she'd heard them nonetheless. As a diplomat's daughter, she'd been trained to listen hard, not just to what was said, but more importantly, to what was implied. Right now, Philippe's amused gaze was telling her he had no other doe in his sight but her.

That dismayed and thrilled her in equal measure.

Switching her attention to her food, she scrambled for reasons *not* to admire this man, *not* to be drawn into his obvious charm or seduced by his intelligence, when he'd had the wit to solve one riddle. Indeed, she had to admit that he had many indications of adhering to her qualifications for a suitable suitor. His clothing, if not borrowed, marked him as a man of some means. He had worthy ambitions and language skills—vital for the fur trade, since the western tribes supplied nearly every single one of the cured pelts that fed the commerce. But she couldn't deny that if she succumbed to the temptation of his crooked smile and dancing eye, this man would make her a winter widow.

She slipped the last bite of ham into her mouth, but didn't taste anything as she dared a sideways look. He sported a strange half smile as he gazed upon her, his plate already clean. When had he eaten? How could she have missed that? And when did Monsieur Bourdon's favorite hunting pup curl up around the legs of Philippe's chair, while Philippe's hand was buried in the pup's fur?

And how in heaven's name had he gotten such a horrendous scar?

No. Mustn't ask him about that. It would be rude to make him self-conscious of it, though his stretching silence and tilted half smile suggested he was waiting for her to ask *something,* and surely every new acquaintance had always asked him about *that.*

"I won't be offended," he said in a low voice, canting a little closer to her, ostensibly to bury his fingers deeper into the pup's coat, but she suspected also to smell her hair pomade or just to let her know he was very, very interested. "I have no secrets, Miss Marietta, and if I did, I sense a woman as perceptive as you would soon sniff them out."

She ignored the flattery. "Of course you have secrets, sir. Every man does."

"You can be blunt, for a diplomat's daughter. And here I was, hoping you'd use those diplomatic skills to try to approve of me a little more."

She laughed. It just bubbled out of her, part cynicism and part surprise. She bit it back almost as soon as it was loosed from her lips.

Too late.

Those blue eyes gleamed with victory.

"What do you think, young man?" Philippe leaned into the table so he could glance past her to Madame Bourdon's son, listening in to their conversation a little too keenly. "Do you think Mademoiselle Marietta is a charming young woman as I do? Did that spontaneous laugh not sound like the joyous laughter of a merry child—"

"My mother wants Marietta to stay forever." Though the boy's cheeks were stuffed with food, he broke into a crumb-dripping grin and glanced up at her through a too-long fringe of hair. "And so do we—all my brothers and sisters. She knows the best games of anyone."

"I'm not surprised." Philippe's voice

dropped an octave. "She knows the best riddles too."

"Yes, oh!" The boy's knife clattered down. "Have you heard this one?"

"Jean-Baptiste," she said, sighing. "This is not the place—"

"I am neither fish nor flesh," the boy interrupted, heedless, "nor anything with a voice…yet when I am born, I make a noise. What am I?"

Marietta squeezed her eyes shut, wishing herself away, willing the laughter at the other end of the table to rise to a pitch that would drown out Jean-Baptiste's glee and no doubt soon-shouted answer.

"Thunder," Philippe declared, teeth flashing. "Born noisy, with a flash of light."

She caught her breath. A quick and clever solution.

But not the right one.

"Nooo." Jean-Baptiste's denial cut through the room's rumbling chatter. "It's a *fart.*"

She shrank in her seat even as Philippe burst into a hearty, chest-shaking laugh of his own, startling the pup at his feet and triggering the laughter of all the people at their end of the table. She was sure Madame Bourdon wouldn't approve of her telling young Jean-Baptiste such an impolite little riddle, but as her face grew warm, she knew she had a reasonable excuse. Upon Madame's gentle request, she'd taken on the task of teaching this boy some Italian. How else was she to convince the energetic young man to stay seated in a chair with a slate when the adventure of the wilderness outside beckoned all young restless souls? She had been forced to use the wit at her disposal, even if it was crude and impolite.

She winced open one eye and saw Philippe's face ruddy with hilarity, his blue eyes fixed on her, twinkling. He was not offended, clearly. What was it about this man, so completely unsuitable in terms of his occupation and plans, and yet so brilliant and clever and kind to dogs and easy with children?

"Come, come." A resonant male voice cut through the hilarity from the important end of the table. "Mademoiselle Marietta, will you share with us what has sent your end of the table into paroxysms of laughter?"

Dear God.

"She is telling riddles, monsieur," Philippe said. "As we all know, this is what our lovely Marietta is wont to do."

"Riddles, is it?" the man said. "Is she sharing *the* riddle with you, monsieur? The one that has stumped every bachelor in Quebec?"

Marietta dared to look up, just as Philippe turned to her, his eyes widening in a dare. She glanced beyond him toward the speaker, one of several administrators who'd made the journey to the settlements with the governor of New France, arriving around the same time as she and the other King's Girls, just this past September. He was an important man in the government, someone whose acquaintance Monsieur Bourdon had been cultivating. A tall, barrel-chested, elegant man with a soldier's sort of straight-shouldered stance, who wore his French-tailored coat quite well. The kind of man with proper plans and occupation, who might be governor himself someday.

Right now, that man was sprawled in his chair, facing her direction while swirling a glass of wine in his hand. Louis-Jacques, yes, now she remembered his name. Early on, he'd come to Madame Bourdon's afternoon soirees. He'd made a point of telling every King's Girl that he came from a rich merchant's family from Poitiers…and then he abruptly, stopped coming to those soirees, even though he hadn't chosen a wife.

Now he looked at her as a silence fell, in expectation.

There was only one way out of this prickly situation.

"I will share the riddle of which you speak, monsieur," she said, raising her voice so it would reach the far end of the table. "If everyone wishes me to."

"I'm sure I represent every unmarried man in the room," Louis-Jacques exclaimed, "when I say we all very much wish to hear it again."

Amid a general murmur of assent, she

gathered her skirts to stand. To be asked to recite was not unexpected. The réveillon meal was usually followed by storytelling and singing and music, and she'd anticipated having to repeat the riddle. Philippe tugged on his short beard as he pushed his chair slightly away to make room for her to stand and step aside. He gave her the slightest nod as she prepared herself to speak. For reasons she couldn't quite discern, that small gesture returned her scattered sense of self-possession.

"Gentlemen," she said, and then, nodding to Madame Bourdon and the other women at the table, "and ladies. I shall recite the riddle, as you requested. Remember to keep your guesses to yourselves, except for the interested gentlemen. The man who solves the riddle is welcome to come courting, if that's his pleasure. As you all know, I am a guest of Madame Bourdon, and the lady receives visitors every afternoon but for Mondays."

She cleared her throat. Amazing how a room full of people could grow as still as an empty church. How her father would be amazed to see the power of their riddles, for he'd never used them except in private, as a game of wits.

She began.

"My first is seen in pillared halls,
Where kings and princes dwell;
'Tis found in every woodland vale,
In every sunny dell."

She paused, folding her hands across her belly, watching brows ripple in concentration.

"Upon the yellow sandy beach,
The ocean billows roar.
"My next—you'll find it in the foam,
Rippling upon the shore."

Honestly, if they hadn't figured the simple key to the riddle by now, it was unlikely anyone would figure out the next three stanzas.

"Within the dark and gloomy cave,
Hid from the sun's bright glare

Precious jewels line the walls
And my third is always there.”

She took a deep breath, bracing herself ahead of the riddle's finish for the inevitable demand for hints and clues.

“My fourth and last is found in France
But never seen in Spain
It has always been in England's clime
In every monarch's reign.”

Would her father have minded that she'd stolen this riddle from her mother, his wife? Marietta had always loved it so, it recited like a piece of poetry. Long ago, when her mother first composed it, Marietta and her father had solved it three days later, almost at exactly the same time. Her father had taken, in his later years, to reciting it often, in memory of this woman they both loved, though it made him melancholy every time.

She took a deep breath and finished it:

“My whole from Jupiter's court on high,

Descends to cheer the earth;
Without his presence there would be
Of happiness a dearth."

There. Done. The silence that followed rang in her ears. Funny, when you know the answer, it seems so clear that you're sure everyone else will perceive it instantly. But that had not been the case, at least not with this riddle, at least among these men.

Her gaze shifted to Philippe, who'd answered yesterday's shorter riddle with such alacrity, but even his averted face was pinched with puzzlement.

Ah. There it is, then.

This riddle kept another bachelor at bay.

So why did she feel a twinge of disappointment?

CHAPTER FOUR

While everyone else in the room contemplated the riddle, Philippe ran his fingers down the back of the dozing pup and studied Marietta.

She stood within arm's reach of him, avoiding his eye while searching the faces of the guests, waiting for someone to speak the solution. The slightest of smiles curved the corners of her lips—how he wanted to kiss that mouth!—but that smile suggested she knew no one present was up to the task of solving the mystery.

How curious.

Perhaps the word puzzle was so difficult as to be unsolvable.

And if it was unsolvable…that meant his lovely Marietta, despite her status as a King's Daughter did not really want to marry.

Suddenly, in the silence, for reasons he couldn't discern, the dream that had been plaguing him leapt to mind. He had experienced the vision every night since he and his Abenaki family had abandoned the northern hunting grounds in favor of migrating to a smoky lodge by the river, to take advantage of the late summer's eel-fishing season. In the reverie, he endlessly tracked a deer wandering through dark woods, a stag that only stopped to circle a rare flower glowing bright in the moonshine.

You came to us seeking, the medicine man had told him, after Philippe had shared the vision. *The dream is reminding you that your search is not yet over.* Upon his advice, Philippe had left his adoptive family and had come to this settlement. He soon found André, who spoke of a long journey west into the moonlit wilderness.

It had all made sense, at the time. But now he faced the puzzle of Marietta.

And this damn riddle.

"Gentlemen, gentlemen," Madame Bourdon announced with a deliberate scrape of her chair as she stood. "Fret not over the riddle. One of you will surely solve it, and when you do, you'll all be clutching your heads over not figuring out the answer earlier. But tonight is Christmas, and our réveillon has only begun. Marietta." Madame Bourdon waved a hand toward the doorway. "Fetch the children from the kitchen, would you? It's time they entertained us."

"Of course, Madame." Marietta bobbed a pretty curtsy. "Isabelle, would you be so kind as to help?"

Philippe heard a rustling of skirts as a slip of a girl—the dimpled one who had made the tourtière—rushed past, following Marietta into the foyer and down the hall to some back room.

"Have you figured out the riddle yet, sir?"

Philippe turned toward the young boy who sat in a chair on the other side of Marietta's. Jean-Baptiste, that was his name, a son of the house. The boy was crumb flecked.

Rough patches stained his cheeks red, probably from drinking too much of the wine he'd no doubt been allowed in honor of the celebration.

"Alas, I haven't," Philippe confessed. "Have you?"

The boy grinned, revealing some food matter stuck between his two front teeth. "I'm still working on it, but I've a notion as to the answer." His eyes narrowed. "Don't try to get it out of me. I won't say a word."

Philippe laughed. "I wouldn't ask."

"She wouldn't respect the man who didn't figure it out for himself," the boy said.

"I know, and yet it's been months and no one has figured it out." Philippe wondered how well the boy knew Marietta and her plans. "I'm beginning to think maybe there isn't a solution."

"Of course there is." The boy looked him over, in the way of a growing young man just feeling the urge to defend his own. "She keeps her word, Miss Marietta does. She knows the solution, and I bet it's a clever one."

"Ah."

"As for me," the boy said, his face flushing deeper, "I'm *glad* Marietta won't court anyone until someone figures it out. I don't want her to get married like all the others. Then she'd leave us! She's the best one to watch over us yet."

Philippe nodded and took the tin cup of wine, but didn't sip. He just turned it around and around in his hand, contemplating what Marietta was up to. A tumble of children stepped into the frame of the wide dining room doorway. Marietta and Isabelle, her little acolyte, shepherded the children into position with low-voiced, motherly skill. A new thought came to him. It wasn't hard to see that Marietta had a generous heart and was of a motherly bent. One glance around the room told Philippe that Marietta appeared to be slightly older than the unmarried King's Girls in the room—or perhaps just more confident by nature. Not just with the children, but also with the fragile-looking Isabelle by her side too. Could she possibly be using the ridiculously hard riddle to hold off her own suitors, while she saw to the happiness of the other King's Daughters?

"Jean-Baptiste."

Philippe startled. In his musing, he hadn't heard Marietta approach. Suddenly, she was in front of the boy. Her tone of voice reminded Philippe of the friar who used to drill him on Latin declensions, though she certainly didn't look like him. Frowning at Jean-Baptiste, she held out to the boy a crown of holly.

She said, "I know you wanted no part of this play—"

"The play," the boy said, scrunching up his face, "is for *babies.*"

"It is not." Marietta waved the crown, urging him to take it. "We need *three* kings, and if you don't fulfill your promise to me, I, in exchange, cannot promise that your mother will allow you to be a part of the revelry on Twelfth Night. You know how much fun that night can be, when we serve up a galette, and we crown a jester…"

The boy plucked the holly-leaf crown from her hand and placed it atop his head with care for the spines.

"In the hall." She pointed toward his

gathered siblings. "Now."

After the boy dragged himself to the doorway, Marietta's glance fell briefly upon Philippe. Philippe felt the tug of that look all the way down to his balls.

He said, "How fierce you are, mademoiselle."

Frowning, she swept away and returned to the children. The nativity play started when one of the bishop's clerks began reading the familiar verses from the Book of Luke. The young girl playing Mary was draped in a blue blanket; skinny Joseph, who by his looks had to be a younger brother of Jean-Baptiste, stood solemn in his brown robes. As the recitation droned on, two of the shepherds in the back began fencing with their crooks, and the little sheep kept wandering about the imaginary barn, but Marietta directed them back to their duties with quiet authority.

Applause erupted as the tableau ended, and the older children, after their bows, moved upon Marietta's orders to take several of the empty platters from the table and carry them down the hall toward the kitchen. In the bustle of the moment, Philippe turned his focus to his friend and found that André's chair was empty. His friend must have slipped out of the room, so Philippe decided to take advantage of Marietta's absence to have a quick word with his business partner. As he stood, he couldn't help casting a glare at the man at the upper end of the table who'd requested that Marietta recite the riddle. Amid the many conversations going on around him, Philippe had caught the man's name—Louis-Jacques something. He wore expensive French clothing and sat in a place of honor, close to the governor. A suitor like that could keep a woman like Marietta in velvet and lace, warm in a fine stone house with servants, and maybe even bring her back to France one day if his ambitions vaulted him beyond what could be achieved in this settlement—

What the hell?

Why was he thinking like this? It had been barely a day and a half since he'd first cast eyes upon Marietta, yet he was still caught in the spell of her presence. He shouldn't be flirting with her, or sizing up rivals. He had plans other than marriage.

Turning on his heel, he left the dining room and headed down the hall, through the kitchen, past the children carrying sweet pies and cakes back toward the dining room, and out the rear door into the frigid, head-clearing air of the Christmas night.

There was André, as he expected. His partner rested one hip on a fence rail. In his hand lay the bowl of a clay pipe, the tobacco glowing inside.

As Philippe approached, André dove right into business. "I spoke to the bishop's man." He held out his pipe, blue smoke curling. "He wants me to come to his office tomorrow afternoon to discuss the voyage we're proposing." André grinned. "We may yet find a source of capital for our ambitions."

Philippe grunted and took the pipe.

"How brilliant you are, my friend." André raised his face to the stars. "Flirting with a King's Daughter to finagle an invitation to the most prestigious réveillon in the settlement, where so many men of means would dine, was a stroke of genius."

"I didn't do it for that."

"Of course you didn't." André barked a laugh. "I don't see you suffering for your sacrifice either, sitting by that gorgeous woman's side. Marietta, is that her name? Smarter than anyone else in the room, if her riddle is any gauge."

Philippe sucked in smoke that made his throat burn. Yeah, she was intelligent. And gorgeous. And sexy as hell. A fine catch for any suitor. The vision of Louis-Jacques passed through his mind, and his stomach clenched.

"Just think." André accepted the pipe Philippe returned to him, and enjoyed another deep draw of the tobacco. "If the bishop's clerk comes through with capital, we'll be well on our way to a September launch of the canoes. Maybe even August. The earlier we head out west, the better, to travel farther before next winter's big snows come." Andre frowned as he stared at the far horizon. "Of course, there's still that matter of finding an agent, someone to store the pelts. I'm not sure about that warehouse fellow we met last week, I don't trust him as far as I can throw him, and he's quite a load to throw. Some enterprising gentleman needs to build a bigger warehouse than his in Quebec, to force that man to charge more reasonable rates…"

Philippe pretended to listen, but this was a liturgy he'd heard before, so he focused instead on a star just above the treetops toward the west. Marietta's gentle face and dark eyes slipped into his mental vision, and the world around him dissolved a little.

Until acrid smoke made his nose twitch.

"You're not listening, my friend." André stood directly in front of him, lit beneath the chin by the red glow of the pipe he was offering to Philippe. "What are you thinking about? It's not the voyage we'll be making, because I just asked you a question about whether to ask the Huron or the Abenaki to make the canoes, and you just stood there staring at the sky instead of arguing for your Abenaki partners—"

"The Abenaki make the sturdiest canoes." Philippe took the proffered pipe and, knowing he wouldn't be able to hide the truth for long, met André's gaze. "I can't stop thinking about her."

Even in the darkness, Philippe saw the flash of pain in André's eyes. Had it been only three years since André's wife had died so tragically, along with the babe in her womb? André rarely spoke of the matter, but Philippe knew his friend well enough to understand that André's silence wasn't forgetfulness. It was his inability to accept the terrible circumstances, and overcome the grief.

Philippe often wondered if André's loneliness was what kept his friend on a wide, wandering path.

André sighed. "You're not thinking of abandoning our plans, are you, Philippe?"

"Of course not." Philippe shook his head. "You know I dreamt of seeking. The elders sent me away from my Abenaki home for this. That's why I am here with you."

André didn't look convinced. "That woman, she's a King's Daughter you know. She's here to find a husband."

"I know."

"They're not suited for our life," André warned. "Not a single one of them, if those women sitting at the table inside are a true representation, can't you see that? What was the king thinking? Quebec doesn't need city-born Frenchwomen."

Like your former wife, Philippe silently noted.

"They'll never survive a place like this. Better to send only farm girls, or even street urchins, if he wants settlers to have families and flourish."

Philippe's throat tightened. Marietta didn't strike him as fragile, unsuited for settlement life, but a woman of such intelligence and wit certainly deserved an easier life than the rough, unencumbered one he had come to embrace, traveling from hunting ground to hunting ground, spending winters in a hut made of poles and tree bark, gorging on a diet of wild berries, eels, and venison. And yet, though he'd embraced that life with gusto, he still appreciated the French ways, the life he'd lived in Dieppe. He still enjoyed customs like this réveillon. He loved the smell of newly baked bread, which he could find only in the settlements. And his heart ached sometimes when he caught the wafting fragrance of a Frenchwoman's perfume.

He ran a hand down his face, weary of all this thinking. He'd been grappling with understanding his place in the world long before his Abenaki father had embraced him as a son. Who was he, really? Was he now Abenaki to the bone, or was he still in his heart a Frenchman?

Or some measure of both?

"God help you, Philippe. You're woman-struck." André groaned as he swung his free arm around Philippe's shoulders. "You know it. I know it. But this relationship can lead to nothing, so let's leave this party before you become even more entangled in those pretty dark eyes. Let's find our pleasure in a tavern."

Philippe conceded, figuring some time away from the woman who'd enchanted him would help him figure things out. He trod around the side of the house with André's arm across his shoulders, keeping his face averted from the windows spilling golden light onto the snow. He closed his ears to the laughter of those inside, and the faint strains of a violin rising…though it played a seafaring tune his feet remembered well.

84

CHAPTER FIVE

Having stayed up at the réveillon until well past three in the morning, Marietta slept until noon, along with everyone else in the Bourdon house, even the children. But since the sun set so early this time of year, once the household finally awoke, Christmas Day was nearly over. They had barely three hours of sunlight for frolicking and visitations from neighbors before darkness descended. Knowing this, the minute the children were awake, she hurried them into their coats and took them outside to play.

The new coating of snow provided much beauty and entertainment. As she watched the children, her thoughts, not for the first time, rehashed the previous interesting evening. The party had been a merry one and a complete success—though, for her, she had to admit some of the joy had drained out of it when Philippe Martineau left after the children's nativity tableau. Louis-Jacques, the handsome and well-dressed administrator who'd showed some interest in her riddle, had quickly taken advantage of Philippe's absence to slide into the seat next to her. He'd been an amusing companion, regaling her with gossipy little stories of political maneuvering in the governor's offices. She'd heard some of these stories before—both Monsieur and Madame Bourdon liked to talk—but Louis-Jacques had kept the tales fresh by adding new details.

She wasn't bored, no…but her mind had wandered.

Her musing ended as the children began whining about frozen mittens and numb toes. She hustled them back into the house, unbundled them, and then shed her own coat and boots. By the fireplace, Isabelle sat in a hearth chair, darning socks. Emilie loitered in a corner with her new fiancé, the young cooper, who'd finally summoned the courage to propose last night. Near the window sat Delphine and the clerk, hands knitted together, framed by a garland of pine boughs, whispering plans for a wedding after the New Year. Delphine's shy young clerk had proposed in the wee hours of the morning, and Delphine was still flushed to the hairline with excitement. Marietta sank into the hearth chair opposite Isabelle, glad for the respite.

But respite was an impossible thing in a house of nine children.

Jean-Baptiste slid around to the front of her chair in his stocking feet, with a ball and a few wooden pins clutched in his hands. "You promised me a game of skittles, Miss Marietta."

"Indeed, I did." She held out her hands to the warmth coming from the flames. "But it's too cold to go outside now—"

"Mama says I can set up the skittles in the hallway." The boy rose to his toes and hurried to add, "**B**ut she said we can't *throw* the ball like we do outside, we can only *roll* the ball down the hallway."

"Your mother doesn't want us to break anything." She frowned. "Or wake the baby upstairs."

"We won't—*I* won't. I promise!"

She considered her options. "There are twelve days to Christmas, you know. We could play outside tomorrow or—"

"But I just got permission!" Jean-Baptiste bounced on his toes, eager to play. "You can't say no!"

She'd have no peace if she didn't acquiesce. "Very well, I'll come to the hallway in a moment, once I can feel my fingers again."

Jean-Batiste darted away. Across from her, Isabelle lifted her head from mending an unending pile of children's stockings and bed shirts, eyes dancing in amusement. Marietta returned her friend's smile and found herself contemplating the one King's Girl left unmarried, other than herself. Isabelle seemed singularly unconcerned about her own lack of suitors. Marietta had wondered if Isabelle wasn't keen on marriage at all. She'd come to believe that Isabelle was just placid by nature, which meant Isabelle would need more than a little help finding a husband.

As feeling slowly returned to Marietta's chill-bitten extremities, Louis-Jacques, last night's handsome administrator, came to mind. Louis-Jacques was eligible and kind, and could certainly offer Isabelle a fine house and plenty of servants. But Marietta doubted she could successfully redirect his attentions away from her and onto Isabelle. Louis-Jacques considered the riddle a challenge. Some men were like that, driven by challenges, preferring to hunt the elusive doe rather than to accept the lovely one standing right in front of them.

Was Philippe like that?

She shook her head. Whyever did that thought pop into her mind? It didn't matter. Philippe was unsuitable for *both* her and Isabelle, because he was a woods runner with an uncertain future and a hard life.

Besides, he'd left the party early, proving he was no longer interested in her.

That was that.

From the hallway came the sound of a

knock on the door. Christmas Day in the settlement, Marietta had come to learn, was a time of visiting friends and neighbors, and since Madame Bourdon had thrown the réveillon, visitors were coming to them to express thanks. Marietta suspected Madame Bourdon was hoping several would stay for supper, for they had a table in the chilly kitchen groaning with leftovers they did not want to go to waste.

Marietta heard a male voice come from the hallway and, at the sound of it, a flush of heat pushed the last of the chill from her body.

She shot up from the chair.

"…Monsieur, it is so good to see you again," Madame Bourdon said. Marietta stepped into the hallway. A strange little thrill vibrated through her. Philippe towered in the doorway, bundled in a fine moose-skin coat and a festive French hat, with a modest, cloth-wrapped package under his arm.

Madame Bourdon's eyes danced. "There you are, Marietta. Look, Philippe Martineau has come to offer his thanks. And he comes bearing gifts!"

"The gifts," he said, in that low, slightly amused baritone, "are for you, Madame Bourdon."

Marietta couldn't hide her surprise. What game was he playing? It was customary to give holiday gifts not on Christmas Day, but on New Year's Day, in less than a week. And yet here he was, arriving like an early wise man. The children gathered around, even Jean-Baptiste, who stood in the hall rolling a skittles ball from one hand to another, watching everything.

And there was Madame Bourdon, mother of nine children, beaming like a young girl. "Why, how gracious of you, sir." Madame Bourdon took the package and squeezed its length. "Is it venison?"

"Indeed." Philippe pulled off a very Parisian hat with a long purple feather and swept down in a bow that took Marietta aback, for it would have been impressive in any king's court, in spite of his deerskin leggings. "In gratitude for last night's feast, I offer you the tenderloins of a newly hunted buck. I can think of no one who can do the venison justice better than you and your talented King's Daughters."

"I shall make good use of them," Madame Bourdon said. "If not this week, then I shall pack them in snow and thaw them for New Year's Day. They will be a welcome addition, fresh roasted, to our New Year's table, to which you are invited, of course."

"My thanks, Madame. I most humbly accept."

Marietta startled. What was going on? Had Philippe come here to finagle another invitation? She'd thought he'd lost interest in her when he left the party last night. She shouldn't care, but there was that wretched thrill again, tingling down her spine.

Madame Bourdon raised her brows to Marietta. "Show Monsieur Martineau into the parlor, would you, Marietta—"

"But Marietta promised to play skittles!" Jean-Baptiste interrupted as the boy slid to her side and took her hand.

"Did she?" Philippe's smile was slow and warm. "Well, Jean-Baptiste, we can't have

Marietta breaking her promise." He crouched and eyed the wooden pins lined up at the darker end of the hall. "I'd be happy to referee your competition, or reset pins, if you'd like. Perhaps the winner can then play me so we can determine a champion?"

Jean-Baptiste shook his head. "You can't beat Marietta."

"Can't I?" Philippe cast her an amused look. "I accept that challenge."

"That's not what I mean," Jean-Baptiste said. "You may be better at skittles, but you can't *let* yourself beat her, because a suitor can't beat a woman in a game when he's courting—"

"Philippe and I are not courting, Jean-Baptiste." Why was her voice so loud? "He has not yet solved the riddle, remember?"

"But he's *here,* isn't he?" Rolling his eyes at the ways of adults, the boy held out the ball to her. "You go first."

"Wait, wait." Madame Bourdon shuffled past them and headed down the dim hall. "Let me put the venison in the kitchen before the balls start flying and I can't get through—"

"One more thing, Madame Bourdon," Philippe said. "Is there any chance Monsieur Bourdon is available for a short conversation today? There is a matter of business I'd like to speak with him about."

"Oh." Madame Bourdon blinked, confused. As confused as Marietta felt, trying to make sense of this man and his motives. "He's in his office right now, but I shall let him know you are here. In the meantime, Jean and Marietta, remember to roll that heavy ball. Don't throw it, and no bouncing. The baby is sleeping upstairs."

"I promise!" Jean-Baptiste said.

As soon as Madame Bourdon turned the corner, Marietta gripped the smooth, hard ball, and, bending deep, sent it rolling toward the pins, knocking down a pitiful few. Jean-Baptiste whooped and darted to the end of the hall to count and reset the pins before Philippe could head down and do it himself.

Momentarily alone with Philippe, Marietta said in a low voice, "So clever you are. Flattering the hostess."

He shrugged. "It is a custom among both

the French and the Abenaki to offer gifts to those who have shared their table."

"It was a kind thing indeed." She drew in a deep breath of the fresh, brisk cinnamon-pine scent that clung to him. "Though one might think you came bearing gifts only for the opportunity to see Monsieur Bourdon on business."

"That wouldn't be true, and you know it, pretty Marietta."

She waited for the bristles she always felt when she was the object of flattery, but they didn't come. "I had no idea you had business with my host. You never said anything about that last night during dinner."

"We've hardly had time to speak to one another about such things." A muscle in his cheek flexed. "My partner and I are in need of trading goods, funds, and advice for the voyage to come, and Monsieur Bourdon is an important man in the colony who may help us attain all three. I'm told this is how grand ventures are arranged."

"I see. I hope your efforts bear fruit, Monsieur Martineau."

He paused a moment, then lowered his head so she felt the warmth of his breath on her head. "You can't possibly believe that I came here just to see *him*, can you?"

Usually, retorts jumped right to the tip of her tongue, but now she found no words there or in her throat.

"You make it hard for a man to get to know you better. You," he added, "and your friend Isabelle. Is that shy young woman in the parlor right now?"

At the sound of Isabelle's name on his lips, a strange, venomous feeling corkscrewed through her. She looked up and found herself much too close to his rugged face. The scar that zagged from brow to chin was narrow but deep, and this close to him, she had the odd sense of staring into a cracked mirror.

He whispered, close enough for her to smell sweet tobacco on his breath. "You're trying to marry Isabelle off first, aren't you?"

She raised a brow. "Is that not the intent of every King's Girl? We were shipped here for the sole purpose of marriage."

"Yes, but you want to see your Isabelle

married and settled before you think of your own future."

His dark blue eyes swam with intelligence. He'd spoken the words in a low voice, but there was no mistaking the meaning. He shouldn't know such a thing. It was no grand secret, but she'd kept that truth to herself because she didn't want to argue with Madame Bourdon or any of the girls about her choice to be the last one to find a husband. That decision, and her strategy to see it through, was nobody's concern but her own.

How unnerving to be so easily read.

"If that's the case," he said, "and by the look on your face, I very much suspect it is, you may want to be a little friendlier to those who come courting. There are many, many suitors interested in you, pretty Marietta. Your riddle is the talk of every tavern. If you were to invite them all in, one or two of them might find relief from their thwarted efforts to court you in the lovely dimple of your accomplished Isabelle."

"My turn!" Jean-Baptiste slid up the

hallway on his stocking feet, the ball held high, oblivious to the sparks lighting up the air between her and Philippe. "Stand back a little, please," the boy insisted. "I need room!"

She stepped away from Philippe and the strange effect he was having on her. She tried to concentrate on Jean-Baptiste, who'd developed a series of exaggerated, preparatory moves that he believed helped him roll the skittles ball straight. But for all her efforts, her mind kept picking over the conversation with Philippe.

He was right, of course. At this late date, with all the King's Girls soon to be married off but for Isabelle and herself, she could allow herself to be more welcoming to suitors. She had offered up the riddle to keep them at bay, which meant she could discard the ruse at her whim. And yet she felt reluctant to do so. The riddle had a dual purpose, after all. She still hoped to find a suitor with the wit and brilliance to solve it.

Multiple pins tumbled just as Madame Bourdon poked her head around the corner. "Monsieur Martineau, Monsieur Bourdon can see you now."

Rescued.

"I'm coming." Philippe gave her a wicked, crooked smile and headed down the hall, tousling Jean-Baptiste's hair as the boy stood up from resetting the pins. "Well done, Jean-Baptiste. Keep up the good work. I suspect I'll be playing you as the champion if you keep knocking the skittles down like that."

The boy lifted his chin and beamed. Philippe stepped over the pins and paused, startling Marietta by turning toward her from the far end of the hall.

"Before I forget," he said, "Miss Marietta, have you heard about the patch of river ice that has been cleared of snow in the lower town?"

She shook her head. What on earth was he talking about?

"They're testing it now, but by the look and color of it, I'm sure it's thick enough for skating. Perhaps the children of the house might want to join me at the riverside tomorrow afternoon and enjoy a few turns on the ice?"

Her heart lifted at the idea of skating, but she hesitated to show any enthusiasm. In any case, he'd invited the children, not her.

"Jean-Baptiste," Philippe said, before Marietta could figure out how to respond, "how would you like to go skating?"

"Oh, yes!" The boy's eyes dimmed. "But only if mother approves."

"Of course, I'll ask her myself," Philippe assured him, casting a glance toward Marietta. "I can be very persuasive."

He certainly could. But she thought it wasn't right to put that idea in Jean-Baptiste's head before speaking to his mother. The boy wouldn't let the idea go if Madame Bourdon refused. Then she realized Madame Bourdon *wouldn't* refuse. Her hostess was exhausted from all the preparations of the season, and there were eleven days left until the Epiphany. It would be a great relief to have all the children out of the house tomorrow so her hostess could plan for the New Year's réveillon, and the gifts for the children, and the marriages soon to follow. Yes, Madam Bourdon would definitely allow a skating party…and yet, Marietta's heart pinched. She wanted to go skating too, and not just for the fresh air and exercise. She dared another look his way, where he stood tall in the dim light at the end of the hall. Philippe, for all his unsuitability, was clever and handsome, and she had to admit that she thoroughly enjoyed his company.

"Marietta," Philippe added, in a lower, huskier voice. "I don't balk at corralling so many children, but it would be a great help to have you accompany us."

Her heart leapt, but she hesitated, her attraction to him battling with her better sense.

"The whole town will be there." He raised a brow. "All the clerks and woods runners will be eager to show off their skills on the ice. Also, I'm sure there will be warm buttered rum available for the weary and the cold. There will be a lot of huddling around a fire. Perhaps we can coax Isabelle into joining our party."

Even across the length of the dim hallway, Philippe's gaze skewered her. She understood what he was implying. There would be many, many eligible men at the event in the lower town, suitors she could put Isabelle in front of, and maybe settle her friend's future sooner rather than later.

So then she could think of her own.

So clever, this woods runner. Subtle as well.

How her father would have adored him.

"We'll see," she said, though her mind was made up. "I can't make any promises until we receive Madame Bourdon's approval."

CHAPTER SIX

Against all of Philippe's expectations,
Marietta came.

Lounging with several other men outside
the log walls of a warehouse, clustered by a
smoky fire surrounded by warm stones,
Philippe grinned with a surge of excitement at
the sight of Marietta in the distance. He
swung out his arm so that his hand, grasping a
tin cup of warm, milky rum, tapped André in
the chest. "Take this."

"Gladly." André grabbed the cup and
squinted over the noisy riverfront looking for
what had distracted his friend. "Who do you
see? If it's the bishop's man coming to talk
business, I'll join you—"

"No need."

"Philippe, you've got a silver tongue," Andre said, taking a quick gulp of the rum. "You've proven that well enough, winning that invitation to the Christmas réveillon, and coaxing a commitment of capital from Monsieur Bourdon yesterday, but I could use a few lessons in those skills so—"

"I'll gladly teach you, but not today. It's not the bishop's man I see." Philippe focused on the slim, bundled figure gracefully swinging her way down the hillside toward the lower town. She was surrounded by a clutch of children so swathed in fur that they could pass for waddling beavers, except they were walking upright. He pulled off his shoulder a marten pelt and tossed it to the young man selling rum. "Make sure these men's cups don't run dry, young man," Philippe told him. "If that fur isn't enough for payment, let me know when I return. I assure you there are more where that came from."

André tsked. "In a generous mood with our furs, are you? Must I remind you that we have many expenses to come?"

"Any gift you grant will come back threefold," Philippe pronounced, another bit of wisdom he'd picked up from his adopted Abenaki father. "There's your first lesson in persuasion, André. Now, gentlemen." He nodded to each of the gathered men, a motley group that André hoped to convince to lend their strong arms and sturdy backs to the upcoming fall voyage. Some, like Wapishka, an old friend of André's who, like Philippe, had been adopted into an Algonquin tribe, had already committed. Others, like the burly, black-bearded Jesuit, Simeon, had only committed in spirit. Simeon was in need of a few compelling arguments to convince his religious superiors to allow him to go.

Philippe stepped away from the huddle and, with his eyes fixed on Marie, wove through the milling crowd, past storefronts and warehouses, past the pile of birchbark canoes ready for tomorrow's ice race, and around merchants sitting on woolen blankets trading furs, tobacco, moccasins, and fur boots, their sleds nearby.

He stopped at the foot of the path,

watching with growing appreciation the swaying way Marietta walked. She'd belted her fur coat, showing off the wisp of her waist and the fine curve of hip. Along with the children, she'd brought her friend Isabelle, proving that Marietta had had the sense to heed his advice. Though why he'd offered it, he still didn't know. His mind hadn't changed about the fall voyage or his reluctance to marry. But his mouth ran ahead of his better judgment whenever he was near this woman. And now that she'd agreed to come, he suddenly remembered that he had a whole new problem to figure out.

He shook off the worry. He'd figure some way around that issue, when the time came.

A small figure broke from the crowd around Marietta and shot ahead in a waddling run. The child's height, compared to the others, gave him away, but still, the boy was so bundled that Philippe couldn't be absolutely sure the figure was Jean-Baptiste until the young fellow raised his face to reveal the spray of freckles around his brow and cheeks.

"Maman said yes!" the boy exclaimed, looking beyond, toward the river. "She even said I could have one small cup of rum, so long as they put lots of milk in it."

"I shall keep that in mind." Slapping a hand on the boy's back, Philippe guided him toward a Montagnais merchant with a pile of footwear on his blanket, as well as skates made from deer shinbones. "Let's get you some skates—"

"No need," came that lilting, intriguingly accented voice.

He braced himself as he turned toward her. The walk down from the upper city had put a bloom of color on her cheeks and a sparkle in those dark eyes the color of oak leaves in autumn.

Hell.

"These children were born in Quebec, monsieur." She lifted from her shoulder a clutch of skates, tied together with narrow hemp rope. "They've been skating since they were old enough to stand. We have a pair for each of them, and even some for me and Isabelle."

"But Marietta, I've *grown,*" Jean-Baptiste insisted. "My last-season skates won't fit me now, I'm sure."

"If that's so," Philippe said, "I shall get you a new pair, Jean-Baptiste."

Marietta sucked in a small breath. "Sir, that isn't—"

"I insist." He patted a second marten fur hanging off his shoulder. "I offered the invitation to all of you and brought trading goods to fulfill my promise."

Her gaze shifted to the thick black pelt he'd sunk his fingers into. "That is quite a valuable pelt, sir. Far more valuable than a few pairs of skates."

"I have many more of these," he said, tilting his head to the warehouse he'd just walked away from. "I am not a man without means, mademoiselle."

Damn his tongue. Around her, he couldn't help himself, even to the point of bragging. Still, he watched her reaction, hoping his boasting had worked to impress. Her long lashes swept down. He wondered, if her cheeks weren't already flushed with exertion and cold, if she would be blushing now at his all-too-obvious flirtation.

Steady, boy.

Steady.

"Here, then, Jean-Baptiste." Marietta separated a particular pair of skates from the bunch slung across her shoulders. She held them out to the boy. "Try these on. Let's see if they fit."

The bundle that was Jean-Baptiste dropped to the frozen ground as he took the skates by the ropes and paired them up against the soles of his boots. The other children, taking their cue, also dropped down, holding out their hands to Marietta for their own skates.

"I suppose," she sighed, "we should all try them on here. The ground is frozen enough that there'll be no harm in walking on them all the way to the river's edge."

"They're too small." Jean-Baptiste rolled back and lifted a foot. "See?"

Marietta frowned. "Indeed."

Philippe held out his hand to the boy. "Come, let's see if that merchant over there has some that will fit you."

She murmured, "Thank you, Philippe."

He paused, Jean-Baptiste's hand in his. Marietta's face, framed by a fox fur hat, softened, and at that moment he realized he'd do just about anything to keep her looking like that.

"But what about you?" she asked, glancing at him up and down. "Don't you need skates, too?"

He shook his head. "Better for me to watch from the shore. Just in case one of the children fall and—"

"No, no." She clucked her tongue. "You must join us on the ice. None of these children is likely to fall, and if they do, they'll bounce, considering how bundled they are. Just because you invited us here doesn't mean you should miss the fun, Philippe."

He imagined her hand in his, her body gliding beside him, and he was lost.

He muffled a sigh. "I'll get skates, too."

Isabelle, watching all this, giggled from behind her muffler before dropping to her knees to help one of the younger children.

From what Philippe had observed, this Isabelle was a fine, easygoing, self-possessed girl, the kind who would make a most pleasant wife for any of the young men swarming on the ice right now. If Philippe himself had come to the settlements for the purpose of finding a French wife, he would consider her a bit too thin and quiet for his taste, but otherwise an excellent option. But he *wasn't* here to find a wife, he *wasn't* here to flirt or to become a settler, he was here because a persistent dream had sent him away from his adopted family to *seek,* and that intent had been thwarted by an early snow and bad luck, and now he had too much time on his hands. He certainly hadn't planned for Marietta or the strange effect she had on him. And yet here he was, trying to figure out how he could push Isabelle into the arms of a suitable husband—he could think of at least three who had new landholdings and, if they had any sense, would welcome such a wife— just to clear his way to court Marietta.

He should stop lying to himself about what he was doing, and what he was feeling.

Dream or not, plans or not, he *wanted* Marietta.

In ways that he absolutely shouldn't.

Grunting, he returned to the task at hand and approached the Montagnais trader. He didn't speak the language very well, so Philippe pulled the marten pelt off his shoulder and presented it to the merchant by draping it over his hands. The trader pinched the thickness of the pelt and nodded in approval. Taking the payment, the merchant spread his hands across the goods on his blanket, indicating that Philippe could choose freely amid all that was displayed.

A moment later, Marietta stepped up beside him with a sigh. "It seems little Marie needs a pair too," she murmured. "My fault entirely. Somehow, her pair was left behind."

"Choose as you will," he said. "I've already taken two pairs, but we have been offered the pick of the pile."

Dropping to his knees on the frozen ground, he measured the shorter skates against the bottom of Jean-Baptiste's boots, and finding them a good size, he tightened the ropes around the boy's booted feet. Then sat back to untangle the ties of his own new set of skates, thoroughly distracted by how Marietta crouched before the merchant's blanket, with the heels of her boots digging into the hard-packed mud, and her skirts taut across her backside, as she picked through the blade-honed bones. He couldn't help noticing how her gaze kept sliding toward a pile of deerskin boots, some lined with fox fur, others decorated with dyed porcupine quills.

Then she turned her head and caught him staring.

"My hostess mentioned," she said, with shyness in her voice, "that the children would soon need to make a trip to the lower town, to be fitted with new moccasins and boots. I can't help but notice that these are lovely and of fine craftsmanship."

"I could offer another pelt." In his head, he imagined his pelt-pinching partner groaning at the extravagance.

"Absolutely not," she said in a voice he recognized better, the stern one she used like a lash. "Thank you for your generous offer, sir, but we could not possibly accept it. Besides, today is not for fussing with impatient young ones while trying on a dozen pairs of shoes and boots, especially when they were brought here on the promise of skating around on the ice, not shopping."

"Wise, as always, mademoiselle."

"And yet I must remember to tell Madame Bourdon to come to this gentleman, if we can find an hour to spare over the twelve days of the holiday."

Philippe, having finally untangled the hemp ties, set the shinbone skates on his soles and attempted to speak to the merchant in his language as best as he could. The Montagnais dialect wasn't so very different from Abenaki, and judging by the trader's nods, they seemed to understand one another well enough.

When he finished speaking, Marietta asked tartly, "What did you say to him?"

"I told him that after the skating is done, he should take his wares and follow you and the children to the home of Monsieur Bourdon."

Her eyes narrowed. "You talked much

longer than what would seem necessary for such a brief message."

"I also said you admired the handiwork of the women of his clan," he added, "and that since children's feet grow very quickly and they wear out shoes quite easily, he would be sure to receive many good pelts from Monsieur Bourdon if he were to make the effort to haul his goods to the upper town."

She paused, thoughts racing across her face, before she nodded. "Thank you for that, sir."

Once their party was appropriately equipped, Philippe stood up too fast and threw out his arms for balance as he wobbled on the keen blades. Jean-Baptiste, who didn't wobble an inch, muffled a laugh and pointed, but fortunately, Marietta didn't notice his awkwardness. Her attention was fixed on the smaller children, some of whom were also wobbling as they made their way across the uneven, rutted ground to the cleared patch of ice.

As they approached the river's edge, Philippe recognized the man sitting on a hardtack barrel right at the edge, observing the skaters. He was one of the barely bearded Rossier brothers—there were seven of them, at last count—and clearly, this one was in charge of the public event.

"Gaspard." Philippe nodded as they neared. "We have quite a large group."

"I see that. The Bourdon brood." Gaspard raised his gaze to Isabelle and then to Marietta, and Philippe frowned at the way the young man straightened from his slump. "Welcome to our little skating party, ladies. I offer you the governor's compliments in honor of the holiday."

"Thank you, sir," Marietta said, drawing Isabelle to her side. "My friend Isabelle and I are grateful for the amusement."

"If only I weren't required to remain here, I would be happy to steady you both on the ice—"

"Gaspard," Philippe interrupted, edging himself closer to Marietta. "Are there rules or can they just step out and skate?"

"Yes, yes." Gaspard gestured toward the wide, cleared patch of ice on the bank of the river, surrounded on three sides by high piles of snow. "The area of ice that is cleared is thick and strong, but you'll notice in several places there are shoveled trails through the snow walls that lead deeper toward the center of the river. Those paths are solely for the canoe races tomorrow—"

"Canoe races?" Marietta interrupted.

"Oh yes." Gaspard's charm flared like a newly lit candle. "Every year during the twelve days of Christmas, we hold a canoe race across this river."

"But…the river is *frozen*."

"In part," he conceded. "That's the challenge, to guide a canoe through the broken ice and drag it over the areas that aren't broken, as fast as possible."

"Goodness!"

"The canoes are all ready, piled up over there." Gaspard turned his head to indicate the tumble of birchbark canoes pulled up on the shore's edge. "They'll set out when the bells of Notre Dame strikes noon tomorrow. The first team to touch the far shore and then successfully return is awarded a bundle of the finest pelts and the pride of triumph."

The children cheered. Philippe felt the sudden intensity of Marietta's gaze a moment before he realized she'd turned to look at him.

She said, under her breath, "You're racing tomorrow, aren't you?"

Of course he was. He and André and Wapishka and Simeon. But he sensed it was prudent to hedge, so he shrugged.

"Such a reckless, mad thing to do." She shuddered and turned her attention back to Gaspard. "Are there other areas of unfit for skating?"

"No, only down those narrow paths," Gaspard conceded. "The deeper you go toward the center of the river, the thinner the ice. It's broken up in the middle because of the current. So for now, children, you must stay in this wide area right here, where we all can see you. No wandering down those paths, understood?"

The children bobbed their heads, straining against Isabelle's and Marietta's grips on their hands to finally get on the ice.

"Very well," Marietta said. "Now that

we've been properly warned, let's join the crowd, shall we?"

Marietta stepped out in front and led them onto the smooth surface, pulling two of the littlest along in a long, steady glide. Jean-Baptiste flung himself onto the ice, his powerful legs—and brashness—propelling him to the far edges, where he trailed a gloved finger through the packed snow walls. The rest of the brood scattered about, some holding hands, weaving through the other skaters.

He stayed where he was, content to watch.

"Monsieur Martineau," Marietta shouted from where she glided in a graceful circle mid-ice. "Come join us, I insist!"

With Gaspard eyeing him, clearly trying to figure out the relationship between him and Marietta, Philippe found himself torn He wanted to be with her. But he also considered he'd make less of an ass of himself if he stayed here and watched the way the breeze toyed with the dark curls spilling out from under her fur hat.

"You're welcome to take my place," Gaspard said with a wicked grin, slapping the rim of the cask he sat on. "I'd be happy to skate beside that fine woman—"

"Enough." Jealously squeezed his innards. "She's with me."

For today, at least. And he'd best get a hold of her hand and let the rest of the men skating around her know she was with him, too. He inched his way onto the smooth ice, avoiding pits, pushing so he would glide toward Marietta with some semblance of grace.

Jean-Baptiste swept by him, skidding on the edge of his sharply-honed shinbones and thus shaving into the air an impressive spray of chips.

"Come out with me, down that path," Jean-Baptiste whispered to him. "That man won't object if you are with me."

"*I* will object." He planted his fists on his hips and used the excuse of scolding to stand safely in one place, balanced, feet apart. "You heard what Gaspard said. The ice is broken midriver, which means it will taper off as you go down that path—"

"Don't you want to impress Marietta?"

Jean-Baptiste grinned as if he were assured of assent. A curl of annoyance tightened inside Philippe. Were all boys this age like this? Philippe's younger Abenaki brother behaved in reckless ways too and spoke challenges to his elders. Like young bucks, risking their own lives by lowering their pitifully small button antlers against a much larger foe.

"Jean-Baptiste!"

Marietta's stern voice cut through the laughter of skaters, the scrape of shinbones against ice, as she came to her own graceful stop by the boy's side.

Saved.

"I heard that," she said in a lower but no less stern voice. "You mustn't even *think* of heading down that path. I will have my eye on you now, be assured, and if I see you even *look* down that path, I will leave the care of the children to Monsieur Martineau and Mademoiselle Isabelle, and I shall drag you off the ice and up that hill, and you can spend your afternoon in your father's study reading a primer upon which I will test you on my return. Understood?"

Jean-Baptiste kicked a rut into the ice but bobbed his head before turning away and weaving between the skaters to a clearer area, where he lingered, scraping sulky circles into the surface of the ice.

"And *you.*" Marietta glided closer, close enough for him to catch a whiff of the womanly warmth of her, rising with the faintest aura of steam from her body. "Tell me you weren't going to say yes to Jean-Baptiste's mad idea."

"I was not."

"I am not convinced." Her rosy lower lip curled a little. "You want to explore those paths. You want to see what you'll be facing tomorrow at the canoe races, yes?"

"I know what I'm facing tomorrow—"

"Breaking through the ice? Going overboard? Getting caught under the ice sheet? Drowning?"

He went very still. "You're worried about me."

She drew herself up, color rising. "I'm worried about anyone who is willing to take risks like that."

"There's skill involved, Marietta." He noticed that her cheeks were reaching peak rosiness, an entrancing sight. "I've traveled hundreds of miles in canoes like those, across white-water rapids and lakes as big as any sea. If you come to watch tomorrow, you might discover that I'm very, very good at it." It was a point of pride for him, how well he'd learned to maneuver a birch bark canoe. There were other skills his Abenaki brothers had tried to teach him, to which he hadn't grasped with as much expertise, but even they conceded he wielded a paddle as well as anyone born to it.

"Skilled or not," she retorted, "a man who'll risk his life for *pride of triumph* would find it very hard, I suspect, to refuse a lesser, if not less risky, challenge from a persistent young boy."

He blinked, surprised. Did she really think he would put a child in danger? *Never.* But perhaps he couldn't blame her for thinking so.

Recently, around her, he'd been driven by urges that did not arise from his thinking mind. Like the urge he was trying hard to resist right now, to lean forward and press his lips against her lovely, plump ones.

Showing Gaspard that she was *his*.

Or would be soon enough.

Then something moved behind those soft brown fathomless eyes, a silver flash of a fish swimming in their depths. Just as suddenly, she glided backward effortlessly, retreating from his reach.

His feet moved of their own accord, and the next thing he knew, they went out from under him. He hit the ice, hard. Even through the thickness of his fur-lined cloak, he felt the impact, jarring his tailbone.

"Philippe!"

He'd closed his eyes in pain, but at the sound of her voice, he winked one open to find Marietta looming over him, lips parted, blocking out the pale blue of the winter sky.

She blurted, "Are you all right?"

"I don't think I broke anything." *Except my pride.* He pushed to a sitting position on the ice, his backside throbbing, trying hard not to grimace.

"Please tell me," she said, breathing hard, "that you paddle a canoe better than you skate."

"A thousand times better, I assure you."

"Oh." She reared back a fraction, still crouched, still balancing effortlessly on her skates, as confusion washed across her face. "Philippe." She blinked, slowly, realization clearing her confusion. "You can't skate."

He sighed. He'd hoped to hide this truth, to muddle his way through the afternoon, but hadn't he already learned that there was no hiding anything from this woman? Certainly not while he was sitting on the ice after that pathetic fall.

"No," he admitted. "I can't skate…not well, anyway."

"But you *invited* us here."

"I did." He didn't dare look over at Gaspard, who'd probably already fallen off his hardtack barrel in paroxysms of hilarity. "I planned to watch you all from the shore, but…"

I can't say no to you.

"That's not rational at all." She shook herself. "You should have told me. I wouldn't have insisted. And how is it that you have great skills at canoeing but not skating?"

"I wasn't born in Quebec like your charges there," he said, nodding to the Bourdon children, now skating circles around them both, grinning and giggling, the girls talking to each other behind their hands. "Skating is purely for enjoyment, but canoeing is *practical*. The rivers are our roads here. Without a canoe, the Abenaki and all the other tribes would rely on our feet to travel between hunting grounds. Not skates." Mortification curled inside him at the thought of his Abenaki family witnessing his clumsiness upon the ice, still. "My Abenaki brothers tried to teach me to skate, but there were so many other, more important skills to focus on, like mastering a bow and arrow, becoming a better hunter, and how to orient in the woods. So I never bothered to become a better skater."

She dropped her hands. Her face cleared

of worry, but he couldn't quite read the expression that took its place, though he liked the way her gaze probed his.

She said, "I'm still baffled why you insisted we come skating."

"It's simple. I want to spend time with you, Marietta."

Well, all his secrets were revealed now. Dissembling might have won him a few more hours in her presence, but he couldn't hold his tongue any longer. He spoke truth, for what it was worth, and he would not take the words back, even if she strode away and left him here, done with him for good. He needed her to know that he was so ensorcelled by her that he would do things he shouldn't do, mustn't do, and couldn't keep himself from doing.

Still, to sit here wounded and confessing his heart was disconcerting, especially since she remained still and silent, maybe a little distressed by his admission.

He determined to change the subject…for now. "How is it that *you* skate so well, Marietta, when you weren't born here either and this is your first winter in Quebec?"

"I lived in the Alps for a while." She fussed with the fingers of her gloves. "My father could speak German, French, of course, and Italian. For a few years, he was a diplomat to part of the Swiss Confederacy. The winters there"—she glanced around, and he got the sense she was avoiding his eye—"they were not too different from the winters here. As a child, I skated a lot on the mountain ponds."

He suspected this was not a confession she'd shared with others, and that gave him a ray of hope.

"Your skill shows," he murmured. "You're the image of grace."

"Nonsense."

She straightened up, as he expected her to. Oh, how she detested flattery.

"I'm rusty, indeed, sir. However"—she held out one gloved hand as she straightened—"I'm not so out of practice that I can't steady you for a careful circuit, if you're so inclined."

He *was* inclined, right down to his sore,

half-frozen ass.

He launched himself to his feet with new confidence. At least she hadn't dismissed him, or taken offense at his words. As long as he could continue to find a way to be beside her, there was hope that someday she'd return his feelings.

He slapped his hand into hers, and let her guide him into a long glide.

CHAPTER SEVEN

The next morning, Marietta tried to talk herself out of going to the lower town to watch the canoe ice races. Madame Bourdon had insisted that the crowd gathered there would be mostly made up of riled-up, probably drunken men who had bet many pelts on one team of canoers or another.

It wouldn't be safe.

Not for the children. Not for Isabelle. Not for herself.

But the children had heard all about the big ice race while skating yesterday, both from Gaspard and from their many friends. They'd woken up begging to go, whining when Madame Bourdon hesitated. Isabelle insisted she would prefer to stay indoors after so much exertion, and Marietta, torn between a senseless urge to be there and the more rational idea to stay home, had remained stubbornly uncommitted even when they teased her—*don't you want to see Monsieur Martineau win?*

No.

She couldn't care less if he won.

She just wanted him to survive.

Even if it didn't make sense to be worried, or to care so deeply about the safety of a man she hardly knew.

So she thought—*no, I won't go*—until she cast her gaze out the parlor window, where the sky was a brilliant shade of blue and no wind swayed the tips of the pines. The white sun shone blinding bright and made the whole world glitter in a way that only happened during the Christmas season, when the snow was still pristine and the air didn't yet bite too hard. The icicles hanging from the eaves dripped a slow drip, proving the day so unseasonably warm that it seemed imperative that she take the children out to walk. How many days like this did they have, before the temperature dropped so low, as Madame Bourdon warned her, that it would freeze their very breath, leave little balls of ice on the tips of their eyelashes? And if they were to walk under this lovely sky, in the midst of the twelve-day holiday, why wouldn't they join the whole of the upper city, well-feasted, eager for distraction, now streaming to the ramparts or down the hillside path to the lower town to watch the races?

Just for an hour, she told herself. Yes, an hour. That was a good compromise. She'd stay until she saw Philippe's canoe return from the far wooded bank and pull up safely on the settlement shore.

Marietta sought out Madame Bourdon in the kitchen, where she seemed to spend all her time these days, and told her that, with her permission, she would take the children to the races.

"I suppose we'll get no peace," Madame Bourdon conceded, as she tossed a washcloth onto the wooden counter, "if we don't agree to go."

"We?" Marietta placed a hand on her arm. "Madame, you must stay here and rest. New Year's Day is coming. Tomorrow, we'll have to start the meal preparations, and then there's the card party for the neighbors in the afternoon. Let me take the children today."

"Oh, I know, but truth be told," Madame admitted, tucking a pale tress behind her ear, "I could use some fresh air. I have been too long standing over this woodstove. Besides"—she leaned in toward Marietta, her green eyes dancing—"my elderly presence as a chaperone will be necessary to protect you and Isabelle from the unwanted attentions of all those rough-and-tumble men…or, at least, give me an opportunity to invite a few of the more sober ones to join us tomorrow for our little card party."

"Join us?"

The party was just supposed to be for neighbors, friends of the Bourdons.

"Come now, Marietta." Madame Bourdon tsked. "You know I have been neglecting my duties to you and Isabelle, but no longer. I've already invited *many* eligible men to join our card party tomorrow, including that handsome administrator, Louis-Jacques de Blanchet."

Marietta took her lower lip between her teeth so she wouldn't frown or show any other kind of disapproval. Earlier in the year, when Madame Bourdon had more than a dozen King's Girls residing in this house, she had made great efforts to attract many bachelors to the parlor for the afternoon. But as the girls were married off and the remaining four proved a great help to their hostess, Madame's attention had returned to the demands of her home and family. So Marietta had stepped into the breach. She reduced the frequency and number of those invitations to be in proportion to how many girls remained unmarried, and also to invite only those interested in the *other* girls, not herself.

But now, facing a weary but determined Madame Bourdon, she realized that—with just her and Isabelle remaining unattached— she could no longer control the situation. The time had come to face what she'd managed to put off for so many months, and choose a man to marry.

Her stomach dropped like she was standing on the deck of a storm-tossed ship. Waves of fear washed over her, fear she hadn't, before this moment, had the courage to admit. She was keenly aware this was the biggest decision of her life. She felt too alone, too adrift, to make it wisely. Just the thought of choosing was overwhelming.

Schooling her face, she nodded to Madame Bourdon, bobbed a curtsey, and then turned on her heel. She would choke down all these unsettling feelings, for now, by setting her mind on the task at hand.

When Marietta announced to the children their decision to go to the ice-races, their shrieks of glee threatened to break the glass in every window. With the noon hour approaching, there was a rush to get everyone bundled and booted and to find hats and gloves that fit and matched. Marietta welcomed the chaos, for keeping her hands busy kept her mind busy, too.

She brought a thick woolen blanket with

her, in case they could find a place to spread it, or in case some of the children became cold. Then, cinching the belt around her own coat, she, Madame Bourdon, and Isabelle stepped out into the blinding sun. Taking their places at each side of the cluster of children and, with Madame behind, they herded the brood toward the path down to the lower town.

Just as they passed a curve in the path, the vista opened to the sight of the St. Lawrence River. The river mostly lay under a sheet of ice covered with pure white snow, but in the middle, rifts both narrow and wide revealed the water, black, swift, and bobbing with chunks of ice. As Marietta drew in her breath, the church bells of Notre Dame rang out through the air, marking noontime.

"It's starting!" Jean-Baptiste, heedless of the ice-scattered path, ran forward in his new fur-lined boots. "Look! They're pushing the canoes over the ice!"

Marietta paused and shaded her eyes. Evenly spaced along the riverbank, a crowd of men started the race by hauling about a dozen birchbark canoes across the cleared area where they'd all been skating the day before. Teams of five dragged each vessel down the shoveled paths that cut through the snow wall, the keels of the canoes leaving narrow troughs in their wake.

"We have to get closer." Jean-Baptiste straightened up to shoot down the path. "Come on."

Trying to keep up without slipping, Marietta walked by the steep edge in order to keep the children in the middle of the road as they all followed in Jean-Baptiste's wake. Below, the riverbank swarmed with men shouting and jumping and cheering. Toward the bottom of the path lingered a denser crowd. Marietta soon realized that viewing the race from the slope upon which she stood held an advantage. From this elevation, they could see all the way to the woods on the far bank. They could also watch the progress of the canoes as the teams approached the fast-moving water in the center of the river.

Jean-Baptiste realized that at the same time she did. He stopped amid a more-thinly populated crowd, just above the large group of observers at the lower part of the path. Pausing to catch her breath, Marietta urged the children to gather and watch the race from here. She shaded her eyes to seek Philippe's team. All the teams were now approaching the dangerous area in the middle of the river, where the water ran so fast that it did not freeze over.

She caught her breath seeing so many men with naked shoulders and bare chests among the teams. At least two of the canoes were manned entirely by men of local tribes, who'd cast off the blankets they usually wore in winter. The teams of Frenchmen, on the other hand, were mostly bundled in leather and furs. She couldn't seem to find Philippe among them.

"There he is!" Jean-Baptiste came up beside her and pointed to the third canoe to the left, which had just reached the rift of open water.

As she watched, the five men of the team synchronized their efforts to step into the belly of the canoe, held bobbing in the water.

She was relieved to see they did not capsize it—and that they completed the maneuver with surprising grace—but at first glance, she doubted that was Philippe's team.

"Jean-Baptiste, I don't think—"

"But it is!" Jean-Baptiste's voice went high with excitement. "I see Monsieur Martineau and that friend of his who came to our Christmas feast—Monsieur Lefebvre, I think. And Gaspard, the man who told us about the race yesterday."

She eyed an unfamiliar dark-skinned man toward the rear of the canoe and a full-bearded teammate on the other side, tonsured like a monk, but the others must be Abenaki or Huron or Montagnais, for their chests were bare.

"Don't you see him?" the boy insisted. "Monsieur Martineau is at the front, at the bow."

Marietta drew in a long, slow breath. As the man at the bow settled into the canoe, Marietta glimpsed a queue of blond hair sliding over a bare shoulder.

Bare.

Philippe wore only a loincloth and deerskin leggings that left his upper thighs naked.

She couldn't fit any more air into her lungs, yet she felt dizzy. She tried to look away. She tried to *think* away. Of course, he would do this race bare-chested. He'd lived with the Abenaki. He followed their lead when it came to canoe-ice-racing. Then it occurred to her that the Frenchmen wrapped in so much hide and fur were at a disadvantage, for the current of the river tugged on the canoes, and some of the vessels wobbled wildly as the men tried to step in and take up their paddles. Imagine the weight of their wrappings, should a Frenchman tumble into that icy water! She'd had horrifying dreams last night about drowning—no. She mustn't think of that, but if she didn't concentrate on something else she might be caught standing here gaping at Philippe's physical beauty, his hard chest, the ripples swelling on his narrow abdomen, the dimples that appeared on his hips when he twisted to check the water on each side, and the tight roundness of his buttocks visible on both sides of his loincloth.

Her body reacted in odd and unsettling ways, low and deep inside.

When she lived in Italy, she'd seen many an ancient statue in the gardens and in the fine homes of the high-born dignitaries her father was required to socialize with. As she grew into womanhood, she'd marveled over such art, but thought they were only statues of gods as the artist imagined them, for they certainly were not made in the image of any man she had ever encountered.

But this man…this man… He was marble come to life.

"Madness, is it not?"

Marietta started and tried to school her face. A man had stepped up beside her. Looking up, she recognized Louis-Jacques de Blanchet, the administrator to the governor who'd asked her to repeat the riddle at the Christmas réveillon.

"It is, indeed," she conceded, breathless for reasons she did not want to admit. "In all my travels, I've never seen the like."

"Quebec is a unique place."

Marietta couldn't tell whether he spoke with admiration or dismay. Perhaps it was a bit of both. It didn't matter, really, she was too addled to make any effort to figure it out. She glanced beyond him to find Madame Bourdon standing at a respectable distance, staring their way with a sly smile. Oh dear. Had Madame Bourdon arranged this meeting? If so, her hostess was wasting no time asserting her matchmaking duties anew.

A ripple of unease shuddered through her body. She lifted the blanket draped over her arm so the wool would cover her chest more completely, as if she were experiencing a chill. She wasn't cold, if anything she felt hotter than she should. She just wasn't ready for such a storm of emotions, from seeing Philippe half-naked on the shore, and now being thrust into company with this man Blanchet, with Madame Bourdon's determined encouragement. She caught her lower lip between her teeth so it wouldn't tremble. She didn't want anyone to know what a frightened little fool she really was.

"This race is a rather rough and rustic custom, but I believe things will change somewhat in Quebec in the coming years," Blanchet mused in that way men did sometimes when they want to give the illusion that they were speaking to themselves as they gazed into the far distance. "Now that our glorious king has taken control of these settlements from that group of merchants that once ran it, everything will soon be different."

"Different?" She shaded her eyes, shifting her attention back to the race because she wanted to and because she couldn't help herself. She caught sight of Philippe and his teammates paddling the canoe in the rift of fast-moving water. "Different in what way?"

"First," he said, jerking a clean-shaven chin toward the race in general, "the king is already making efforts to get those good, strong, but often rootless young Frenchmen to stop racing canoes and start clearing ground instead."

That wasn't anything new, she thought wryly, for as a King's Girl, she'd been brought here to settle one rootless young Frenchman herself.

He continued, "It's a necessary change. The settlement can't live forever on goods shipped from France. It needs farms."

"I see."

She didn't really, because Philippe's canoe was being dragged downstream by the current rather than being paddled straight across the open water toward the far bank, where all the other canoes were heading. Several of those teams were already hauling their canoes on the solid areas of ice close to that far bank. Why was Philippe's team paddling the canoe parallel to the far shore, instead of heading straight at it?

What was he thinking?

Louis-Jacques was still speaking. "The problem with having merchants manage these lands and these settlements, as they did for thirty-odd years, is that they were solely concerned with nothing else but maintaining the fur trade."

"The fur trade."

She repeated his last words, an old trick of hers, because she didn't want to be rude but she wasn't really paying attention. Instead, she pressed her palm against her chest, for her heart was racing much faster than the canoe she was watching, heading dangerously fast downstream.

"Mark me, the fur trade has brought the crown great value," Louis-Jacques said, "but King Louis has greater ambitions. So there will be…changes."

She bobbed her head though Monsieur Blanchet's words sounded like a mosquito-whine in her ears, for Philippe and his team suddenly back-paddled toward a narrow finger of solid ice that jutted into the current of the river. To her untrained eye, the narrow isthmus of ice looked solid straight to the far bank, and clear of the kind of snow drifts that were slowing the other teams' efforts to reach the wooded edge. But what did she know of such things? With an unearthly grace that barely wobbled the vessel, as well as a ripple of gleaming, muscular shoulders, Philippe shifted out of the canoe and onto the ice, testing the surface before seizing the bow of the canoe so the other men could disembark.

She dug her fingers into the woolen blanket as all the men leapt out of the canoe without incident, and the team began dragging the canoe over the ice. In the brief moment of relief, she realized that Monsieur Blanchet had gone silent.

Silent enough for Marietta to suspect that she'd given away her inattention.

She cleared her throat and said, "Do you have a favorite in this race, Monsieur?"

"I'm not a betting man, Mademoiselle."

"That is a fine quality," she conceded. "And yet still, without wagering, you might have a favorite."

"I think you might too."

She pulled the edges of her hood closer to hide her blush. She'd been too obvious. And how foolish was she, acting like a flighty fourteen-year-old rather than a wiser, much more sensible twenty-four-year-old. A twenty-four-year-old who knew the man now racing shirtless across the ice could not give her what she really wanted.

Stability. Constant companionship.

A sober and serious husband.

Like Louis-Jacques, who had fixed himself at her side. He deserved consideration, now that she couldn't put off a decision about marriage much longer. She looked up to find him smiling down at her, and she forced herself to look at him as a suitor. Louis-Jacques de Blanchet was tall, not too young or too old, fit in the flat-bellied, straight-shouldered way of a soldier. He wore a buttoned, knee-length woolen coat of fine construction and tailoring, his hat fur lined and sensible, with only a single feather as a nod to current fashion. His face was clean-shaven in the old French way, with the slightest of mustaches. His eyes were the same dark brown as his long, queued hair, and there was patience, consideration, and intelligence on his face she couldn't deny.

But for the endless political talk, Louis-Jacques would be quite a good husband. But right now, maybe because she did not know him so well, or maybe because there was a half-naked other potential suitor distracting her, there was something about Monsieur Blanchet…something she couldn't quite pin...something *missing*.

"Mademoiselle," Blanchet began, a ribbon of hope in his voice, "Madame Bourdon has just invited me to a card party in her parlor tomorrow. She assured me you would be there."

"Yes," she said, her throat tightening. Her gaze shifted back to where it wanted to go, to where Philippe and his team had reached the far bank, only to turn the canoe around to drag it across that finger of ice once more, toward the rift of swift-moving water he'd have to cross over again. "Yes," she repeated, "I will be there."

"I'm glad, mademoiselle." Blanchet said. "You are a cipher, as intriguing and difficult to understand as your riddle."

"I shall take that as a compliment, sir."

"It was meant as one."

She ignored the flattery, for Philippe's canoe was back in the water, and he and his team were paddling hard against the current. Her breath came short as she watched the muscles of Philippe's arms flex each time he dug his paddle deep, his chest bellowing with exertion. Bathed in an unsettling tingling feeling, she pulled her gaze away from all that naked flesh to what else was happening on the water and ice. Apparently Philippe's team's earlier, odd strategy had allowed them to surge ahead of several canoes. Philippe's team wasn't in first place as they pulled up to a solid ice sheet and began the dangerous shift from canoe to floe, but they were an easy third. They were still working on shifting on solid ground when a shout of triumph rose from the crowd on land. The first team had bolted with incredible speed to finally reach the shore and win. The second team sprinted up only moments behind. The men of the winning team danced about on land, celebrating with warbling cries of triumph.

She noted that one of the two teams of Abenaki or Huron had won the race, followed by a team Montagnais, she assumed, for she recognized one of the teammates as the trader who'd sold the Bourdon family new boots and moccasins yesterday. The race done, she allowed herself to check how Philippe's team was doing, and saw them, too, right behind, sprinting to the shore with the canoe between them…but something wasn't quite right.

1…2…3…4….

She counted only four men.

Her heart filled her mouth when she realized who was missing.

"Dear God in Heaven." She followed the rutted trail of the dragged canoe to glimpse a figure halfway in the dark water, hauling himself out onto the ice.

"I must go," she said, struggling not to sound too panicked as she tightened her grip on the blanket draped over her arm. "That man is likely to freeze."

Ignoring Louis-Jacques's bark of surprise and Isabelle's quiet gasp, Marietta darted her way through the crowd, stuttering apologies as she shoved a shoulder through the gathering at the base of the path. She finally broke free onto the stretch of the lower town that smelled of smoke and ash from bonfires. She crunched her heeled boots deep into the ground so she wouldn't slip as she flew across the shore, passing by the winning canoes. Ahead, she glimpsed a dripping, shivering

Philippe, now slumped in the grip of his crewmates, who'd gone back to haul him across the ice where they'd all skated yesterday.

"There's a bonfire over there," Marietta blurted, pointing in the direction of a blaze not far away. "Bring him there. And fetch some rum!"

The men shifted direction and headed where she told them to go. Philippe's lips were turning blue, his arms looked ice burned, and his limbs limp. In spite of all that, he was smiling.

"Third place, fellows," he mumbled. "And only one of us ended up in the water. A respectable showing—"

"Shut up, you." A wild anger filled her. "You could have died, you fool, and you may still."

"You're here." His bleary gaze shifted to her, and the puckered scar on his face stretched as he smiled. "My angel."

The men laughed at the fancy and set him down by the fire, not as gently as they could have. She shooed them away and crouched beside him, unfurling the blanket she'd brought, rolling his gleaming, half-naked body in it until he was properly cocooned and as close as he could get to the fire without going up in flames himself.

"Where's that rum I asked for?" She raised her head and glared at his gathered teammates—such a varied crew, a tattooed African, a Jesuit in a tunic of brown wool, the too-young, nearly beardless Gaspard she'd met yesterday, and André. "Well?"

Gaspard shot off toward a warehouse while the others just looked sheepish, casting gazes toward the revelry happening by the shore as the canoe teams came in, one after another.

"Oh, go on, the rest of you," she insisted. "Celebrate as you will, now that you've all defied certain death."

They scattered like geese.

"Next time," Philippe muttered, the words shivering as hard as he was, "you should lead the team—"

"I have more sense than that."

"They responded to you better than me,

or at least Gaspard responded more quickly." He raised his shoulders from the ground and sat up. "I fell into the water because Gaspard didn't understand my orders—my fault, in the heat of the race I spoke Abenaki by mistake—it was a miracle the canoe didn't capsize on us all. Ah, and here he is, unable to keep his eyes off you."

Gaspard suddenly appeared beside her, breathless and flushing to the roots of his hair. From Philippe's teasing, no doubt.

"Thank you, sir," Marietta said as she took the tin cup of rum he offered. She turned to place it to Philippe's lips. "Stop teasing him and drink this."

He offered a sliding sideways smile before he drank. Gaspard set off to join his friends, she supposed, for she heard only his swiftly-retreating footsteps.

By the time Philippe lowered the cup, his lips were no longer blue and his harsh breathing had subsided. He'd managed to muscle his ropy, naked arms completely out of the blanket, and drape them over his knees, as if oblivious to the cold.

His blue eyes fixed disconcertingly on her. "You came to watch me race."

"Hardly." She kept her gaze somewhere above the ruddy flesh of his shoulders and chest. "The children clamored to come after hearing you and Gaspard talking about the races."

"And you always listen to the children?"

"I am outnumbered, you know."

"And yet they'll do anything you say." He tugged the edge of the blanket closer to his chin as he set the tin cup down. "What luck that you brought a blanket for me."

"What idiocy that you did not."

He shrugged. "I didn't intend to take an ice bath."

"And yet you put yourself into a situation where it was very, very likely you would—"

"I'm fine, Mademoiselle. Healthy and alive. Though I wish we'd won." He squinted beyond her to the celebration at the shore. "That Abenaki team wins this race almost every year. Still, I tried, because I had my eye on a valuable prize."

She resisted the urge to roll her eyes. "A

pallet of pelts?"

"Your admiration."

Dear heavens, he was doing it again, speaking with a rashness she didn't know how to manage. And why would he think she would admire his racing, anyway, when all she'd done from the moment she'd learned about the races was scold him?

And yet here he sat before her, grinning after being half drowned. She'd never known anyone with such carefree daring. In only moments, he'd shrugged off the shock and the fear. He'd lost the race but bore no one ill will, not the winners, not his team who he'd probably sent ahead to finish the race as he'd struggled out of the water. He wasn't even angry at Gaspard. And amid all that had just happened to him, he still summoned the nerve to *flirt* with her, sitting here on the ice-crusted, muddy-rutted ground.

What kind of man was this? She was a diplomat's daughter. She assumed everyone was always lying, hiding secrets, burying their true motives beneath a mask they thought you wanted to see. But there was not a drop of dissembling in Philippe Martineau right now. She wasn't sure she'd ever met anybody who so boldly revealed his true self. That true self was undeniably a man of wit and courage, recklessness and raw intelligence, and, above all, bountiful good humor.

In her heart surged a reluctant admiration.

"Tomorrow," he murmured, raising his knees and leaning into them, "some of the men plan to carve a slide down the slope. They do it every year for the children. For the town. Come and ride with me."

In her mind, she felt his strong chest at her back, his arms wrapped around her, his legs spread out on either side of her hips as they slid down the ice together, falling in abandon and on the edge of control, the wind riffling through her hair.

Her whole body tingled at the idea, in a new and wicked and wonderful way. She wanted to say yes, yes, *yes.*

Instead, she heard herself say, "I can't join you tomorrow."

His smile dimmed. Her heart squeezed at the sight. Dear heaven, what had this man done to her? She had no control over the way he made her feel, and those feelings were strong and contradicted better sense. She had to *think*. She had choices to make, hard choices that would affect her entire life, and she had to find a way to make the wisest decisions, and choose the right man.

"Why can't you come to the slide?" he asked.

She shook her head. "I have another engagement."

"Cancel it."

"I can't. It's happening where I live. Madame Bourdon is hosting a card party." She rose to her feet, putting some space between herself and this puzzling man who affected her so strongly, who she definitely needed to know better. "Come join me tomorrow, Monsieur Martineau. I'll save you a seat at my table."

CHAPTER EIGHT

During the whole climb that led to the upper town and Madame Bourdon's home, Philippe argued with himself.

He ached to be with her, but a better man wouldn't have accepted her invitation. He had nothing to offer this woman, nothing that she wanted, but he simply couldn't think beyond his need to see her. Marietta had even shifted into his dreams. Last night, instead of the usual dream of following a stag into the blue evening woods, a deer in search of a rare, moonlit flower, he'd had a completely different and more vivid dream of his own soil-flecked hands piling stone upon stone upon stone. Odd. If his people weren't so far away roaming the hunting grounds south of the St. Lawrence River, he would seek out his Abenaki medicine man to make some sense of this new vision, because he couldn't read it, not in the state he was in. He couldn't even make sense of his waking behavior, as the urge to see her, to be with her, grew ever more powerful.

And now here he was, knocking on Madame Bourdon's front door, the same door he'd stopped not far from, stunned into attention less than a week ago, as Marietta emerged from it in a blue woolen coat with marten-fur trim.

"Monsieur Martineau!" Madame Bourdon swung open the front door herself. "You are just in time. We were all hoping to play several rounds of brelan, but we lacked one more person to form the last foursome."

Philippe smiled. The card game brelan could be played with three or more people, so there was no real reason for a fourth. Madame Bourdon's little speech was a subtle but agreeable way to say *welcome, I should have invited you myself, but all's well now that you're here.*

"I'm returning this, Madame." He thrust at her the woolen blanket Marietta had wrapped him in yesterday, now brushed free of mud and debris. "I'm looking forward to the opportunity to thank Mademoiselle Marietta for the health of my toes, for I believe her quick actions helped stave off frostbite."

"Indeed! We were all worried when we saw you tumble into the river." With a shake of her head, Madame Bourdon took the folded blanket from his hands and then stepped aside so he could enter. "Her card table is in the back, with an empty seat."

He nodded, pounding the mud and ice off his turned-cuff boots, purchased for the occasion, and stepped into the foyer ablaze with candles to divest himself of fur hat, thick gloves, leather belt, and fur-lined coat. He noticed Madame Bourdon's assessment as he peeled down to the velvet coat he'd sent to be tailored just for this afternoon call, and the woolen hose beneath. He preferred buckskins and leggings when out in the Quebec weather or when hunting or laboring, but there was much to be said for French fabrics. Like this, as in so many things, both physical and philosophical, Philippe appreciated and admired the luxuries he'd never experienced during his French upbringing and the practicalities he'd adopted from the Abenaki in equal measures.

With Madame Bourdon's urging, he stepped into the parlor, where a fire roared. The furniture had been moved against the walls to make space for a half dozen tables, where the gathered guests—four women, as far as he could tell, and close to twenty men—turned in unison when his booted heel hit the wood floorboards.

He bowed as regally as he could manage.

"May I introduce Monsieur Philippe Martineau, for those who might not yet be acquainted," Madame Bourdon announced to the crowd in general. "Your table is over there," she urged, nudging him deeper into the room.

He glanced over, but Marietta turned her

face away at the same moment, and as he wove his way through the tables, he found himself mentally urging her to glance over her shoulder again, as he stared at her gleaming black hair, styled in a tumble of sausage curls that fell across bare shoulders that stiffened so tightly that the hem of her off-the-shoulder sleeves dug into her skin.

Was she nervous? Shy? He couldn't tell. She kept her gaze firmly on the cards she shuffled as he rounded the table to take his seat. Only then did he notice the other players at the table, the dimpled, well-tempered Miss Isabelle…and, with a jealous twist, he noticed the man across the table was one of the new governor's most esteemed administrators, the man from the Christmas réveillon, the one who'd insisted Marietta recite the riddle.

"Monsieur Martineau," that man said, breathing deep to put some strain on the brass buttons of his fine coat. "We have not been officially introduced." He held out a hand, lace dripping from his wrist. "I am Louis-Jacques-Francois-Martin-Laurent de Blanchet, recently of Poitiers."

Oh, the temptation to offer his Abenaki name.

"Philippe Martineau, recently of Dieppe." Philippe gripped the other man's hand so they met in the middle of the table, noting how smooth skinned—but not feeble—it was. Philippe said, "I hear you're one of the governor's men."

"I am." Louis-Jacques retracted his hand. "Pity about the canoe race yesterday. Losing and all."

"We made a respectable showing." He glanced at Marietta, still shuffling cards, her gaze still cast down. "And I had the pleasure of having Miss Marietta save me from what might have been a severe case of frostbite with her quick application of a blanket…and rum."

The man's dark eyes flickered in the candlelight as Marietta nodded, acknowledging his appreciation. She remained demure, silent, and looked somewhat pale.

"Shall we play, sirs?" Marietta dealt the cards with a casual deftness. "I assume you all know the rules to brelan?"

Phillipe tapped each card as it slid before him, his attention on the man opposite him. "Are we not supposed to wager first?"

"There will be no betting, not here." Marietta tilted her head toward Louis-Jacques. "Monsieur Blanchet is not a betting man."

Philippe murmured, "Isn't he?"

Louis-Jacques swept up his cards. "I find the urge to win wealth rather than to earn it, quite distasteful."

"Wagering," Philippe said pointedly, "elevates an idle game, in my opinion."

"If you came here wishing to wager," Louis-Jacques said, "you'll be more than welcome at one of the other tables, Monsieur Martineau. By the sound of the cursing, there are many men willing to offer up their chairs."

"I'll stay nonetheless." He smiled in a way that he suspected looked wolfish because of his scar. "This table has the benefit of two lovely King's Daughters."

Isabelle made a nervous little giggle, and Marietta frowned at him. He held her gaze, transfixed by those fathomless dark eyes, flickering with more than a reflection of the room's many candles. But he saw a reserve in them. He wondered what happened to the encouragement he'd witnessed yesterday, when she'd unexpectedly invited him here. He slid a look at Louis-Jacques and wondered if Marietta was putting them both to some sort of test.

She was such a riddle.

"Speaking of earning wealth," Louis-Jacques ventured, as he frowned at the three cards in his hand. "I understand that you are planning a trading trip into the interior, Monsieur Martineau."

How did this man know about that, unless Marietta had mentioned it? It was a sore subject. Despite their recent efforts, he and André kept stumbling upon difficulties, and in Marietta's presence, he preferred not to talk about his upcoming travels.

He kept his answer brief. "In the late summer," he conceded.

"Seems like a waste of your efforts," Louis-Jacques said in a half-distracted way, "when the western tribes, through their middlemen, the Hurons, already bring the furs to Trois-Rivières and Montreal themselves to trade."

"You are new to the settlements. Perhaps you are not so familiar with recent events." Philippe switched his cards around and tried to concentrate on strategy. "The Huron's blood enemies, the Iroquois, have been making raids from the south in an effort to exert some control over the fur trade and funnel the land's wealth to the English and Dutch."

"I'm very aware of those developments, I assure you." Louis-Jacques leaned back and ran a finger over his trim mustache, his gaze focused on his cards. "In fact, among other duties, the governor has tasked me with drafting a letter to the king himself, requesting a regiment of soldiers to be sent here to be allies of the Huron, help them defend the routes and the trade, and discourage such attacks."

"It could take years for that to happen." Philippe wasn't sure he liked the idea either. The presence of soldiers tended to cause trouble rather than allay hostilities. "In the meantime, our venture will allow the trade to continue for the benefit of all, and at the same time permit the people of the Huron and the western tribes to avoid conflict with their enemies."

"For all the logic in your argument," Louis-Jacques conceded, "it does not completely align with the will of our most sovereign king—"

"Isabelle," Marietta blurted, raising her face to meet the gaze of her quiet friend right across the table. "Isn't it vexing when gentlemen delve so deeply into conversation on matters of trade—or government—when they have not been encouraged to, in the middle of what should be a pleasant party?"

Isabelle made a little gasp, fiddled with the cards in her hands, and lowered her lashes as she chewed on her bottom lip.

"Since I dealt the cards, Monsieur Martineau," Marietta said, clearly not expecting a response to her remarks from her friend, "and you are on my right, it is your turn to let me know if you'd like to exchange any of your cards for new ones."

"I'll hold," he said. She could lead a regiment of soldiers, this woman, and win the war with a single glance.

He was a lost man.

Irrevocably.

As it was her turn, Isabelle passed two of her cards over to Marietta, and Marietta replenished Isabelle's hands with two new cards. A contemplative Louis-Jacques exchanged only one, and finally, Marietta exchanged two of her own.

"So," Marietta said, placing her hand facedown. "Shall we require a second round of card exchanges, or would you all prefer to play only one round per game?"

"If I may," Louis-Jacques interrupted, leaning into the table, "I would like to propose a wager."

Philippe couldn't help himself. "You announced only moments ago that you would find betting distasteful."

The administrator shot him a dagger of a glance. Philippe was mildly astonished at the fierceness of it. Perhaps he was facing a more worthy adversary than expected, in many ways.

"If I win," Louis-Jacques continued, "then I will demand that you, Marietta, grant us a recitation of that riddle again."

"Oh, how foolish a wager, sir." She waved a hand in the air as if wishing away Louis-Jacques's words. "Why must I always repeat it? It's my understanding that the riddle has been memorized by many, and one gentleman told me that the riddle in its entirety has been scrawled on the wall of one of the lower town's taverns—"

"But we're not in a lower-town tavern, miss," the ass persisted. "I very much want to hear the riddle fall from your own lips. There is hidden meaning in intonation, and emphasis, and it might help me solve it."

She frowned, contemplating, and, jealous that she would take such notice of his words, Philippe blurted, "And should you lose, monsieur? What do you offer in return?"

"Should I lose," he drawled, tearing his attention from Marietta, "I'll accept any reasonable wager that the winner, whether you, Miss Isabelle, or Miss Marietta, would suggest."

Philippe's suspicion swelled. Either the man was a fool to potentially place that kind of power in Philippe's hands, or more likely, his rival had a very, very good hand.

"I say we take the good gentleman's wager," Philippe said, glancing at his own cards, "but only if we allow a second round of exchanges."

"Very well." Marietta's gaze slid between the two men. "I suppose there's no harm in that wager. If you agree to Monsieur Martineau's terms, Monsieur Blanchet."

"Agreed." Spoken like the flash of a rapier.

"Monsieur Martineau," Marietta said in a firm voice. "How many cards?"

"I'll hold."

His opponent across the table didn't look pleased with that answer.

"Isabelle?" Marietta asked before sliding one card across the table to her friend and retrieving the discard. "And now you, Monsieur Blanchet?"

"I'll hold."

The words hit him like the cut of air from a swift-moving blade. Philippe realized he was going to lose this wager. It shouldn't matter, the consequences appeared to be nil, but Louis-Jacques was up to some mischief, and Philippe couldn't figure out what it was.

"I'll hold also." Marietta placed the remaining deck next to the overturned card in the middle of the table. "Shall we show our cards in the same order?"

Philippe turned over his cards to reveal a pair royal, a hand of high value and caught the gleam of triumph lit in his opponent's eye. That meant—as he moments later discovered to be true—that the administrator had a brelan carré, four of a kind, the three jacks in his hand matching the jack in the center. No hand was of higher worth than that, which rendered Isabelle's and Marietta's cards irrelevant.

"Well," Marietta said, tossing her cards in the center. "I'm glad that's at an end, at least. If the game had gone on any longer, I feared a duel might break out."

Philippe slid his cards to the center,

feeling a bit sheepish. Maybe because she was so skilled with disciplining unruly young boys, Marietta had a way of making others well aware of their bad behavior without completely calling them out. By the look on his rival's face, the sheepish feeling was mutual.

The table rattled against the wooden floor as she suddenly stood.

"Ladies and gentlemen." Her voice cut through the murmur of conversation and shuffling of cards throughout the room. "I have lost a wager and have chosen to fulfill its terms immediately. If you all would be so kind as to finish your current hand, I will then, by the command of Monsieur Blanchet here, who won the wager fairly, accede to his request to once again recite the riddle you all know so well."

There was a hurried rustle of cards, a movement of chairs, and low conversation as hands were finished all across the room. Marietta, chin raised, paid no mind to him *or* Louis-Jacques, just stood straight as a post, her hands half buried in the dark blue folds of her voluminous skirts, watching and waiting patiently.

"Very well," she said, as the rustling of clothes and wobble of chairs ebbed and the room settled in expectation. "I shall begin."

My first is seen in pillared halls,
Where kings and princes dwell;
'Tis found in every woodland vale,
In every sunny dell.

Upon the yellow sandy beach,
The ocean billows roar,
My next—you'll find it in the foam,
Rippling upon the shore.

Within the dark and gloomy cave,
Hid from the sun's bright glare,
Precious jewels line the walls,
And my third is always there.

My fourth and last is found in France,
But never seen in Spain;
It has always been in England's clime,
In every monarch's reign.

My whole from Jupiter's court on high,
Descends to cheer the earth;
Without his presence there would be
Of happiness a dearth.

Philippe listened to her clear, distinct recitation but hardly heard the words. The riddle was impossible, he had been long convinced. Any man who had any hope of winning this woman's heart would have to find ways to woo her in a fashion she didn't expect. And so while she spoke, he watched the way her throat moved, the depth of the hollow rising and falling, the slim length of her clavicles becoming more pronounced as she continued through the stanzas, and vowed that someday, he would lay kisses upon that throat, run his jaw across her clavicle, bury his nose in the little hollow at the base of her neck.

In the brief silence that followed her recitation, he shifted on his seat, grateful for the length of his velvet coat that hid his excitement.

Then a chair scraped and the table wobbled again as that wretched rival of his, Louis-Jacques, ruined the moment by standing up, spreading his arm to show off the lace at his wrists, and bowing deeply before Marietta.

What a peacock.

"Mademoiselle Marietta," the ass said in a voice loud enough to reach the corners of the room. "Thank you for that lovely recitation."

Marietta bounced in a short curtsy. He saw the motion out of the corner of his eye, for he sensed a new danger emanating from his slyly smiling rival.

"If Miss Marietta will permit me," Louis-Jacques said, straightening. "I will announce the answer, for I have solved the riddle."

CHAPTER NINE

"Sir." Marietta grasped the back of her chair in a way that she hoped didn't give away how desperately she needed the support. "If you know the answer to the riddle, then by all means, speak."

Louis-Jacques's sudden smile made him look less guarded, less officious, more boyish. The effect should have been charming, but it brought her no pleasure. The idea that he'd solved the riddle unsettled her. Perhaps she'd become complacent as the months went by and no man even came close to unwinding the word puzzle. The riddle had been a high-walled, impenetrable palisade, protecting her from the hard decision she would inevitably be forced to make.

Perhaps now.

Today.

"The answer is quite simple," Louis-Jacques announced, "but the reasoning necessary to understand is not, so please indulge me as I explain my solution by its parts."

She nodded briefly, but didn't dare look at Philippe, still seated at her right, though she sensed his stony stillness.

"The first stanza," Louis-Jacques explained, "represents power, which we all know resides first and foremost in the 'pillared halls' of kings and princes, but also, by good administration, it permeates every woodland field and sunny dell."

Marietta drew an imaginary veil of stone over her face so she would not give away her thinking as her mind raced down a thousand paths.

"The second stanza," her soon-to-be suitor continued, turning toward the crowd with the air of a seasoned speaker, "refers to yellow sandy beaches, ocean billows, and the foam that ripples upon the shore—*this* shore, this grand and beautiful wilderness separated from France by the wide sea, a place of tremendous wealth in many ways, which is the second source of the power heretofore mentioned."

With Louis-Jacques focused on the other guests, she couldn't help herself, she glanced down at Philippe to find his face a mask. Why she even had such an urge to look at him was beyond her understanding—these past days, Philippe had been persistent and witty—and reckless and lively and wonderful—but she had dismissed him from the first as an unsuitable suitor, because he was a woods runner who would leave any wife as a winter widow. That had not changed, and thus neither should her opinion of his suitability.

"The third stanza speaks of a dark and gloomy cave that yet has precious jewels within and that, as you all are likely beginning to surmise, represents the many religious houses both here and in France where monks and religious sisters labor, often cloistered, to do glittering good works. That is the third source of the power heretofore mentioned."

She closed her eyes. *Think.* Louis-Jacques was clearly convinced that he'd won permission to court her. She should be excited, for the riddle had worked, in its way, drawing to her someone with intelligence and a flexibility of mind. And Louis-Jacques was a fine man. He suited her in the important ways. He was a man of means. He could easily provide for her and the children they might have. She admired the man's ambition, his placid temperament. Also, he'd been solicitous of her, never pushing his suit, needling her for hints, or drowning her in flattery. Life was unpredictable, but it was unlikely that the wife of Louis-Jacques would ever have to count dirty *sous* to pay the butcher before their credit was cut off. A wife of Louis-Jacques would never have to turn shirt cuffs to hide the fraying or, driven by hunger, time their visits to old acquaintances in order to increase the likelihood that they might be invited to dinner and have a chance to eat for the first time in days.

And yet…listening to Louis-Jacques'

explanation, she realized his solution hadn't completely removed her power of choice.

"The fourth stanza," he continued, "is the trickiest of them all, in my opinion. I must compliment Miss Marietta"—he turned to look at her with a bow of his head—"for being so well educated on this subject. The stanza refers to the many merchant's organizations that have, now and formerly, encouraged trade and exploration around the world. The 'last,' as the stanza says, is found in France, and that refers to the Company of One Hundred Associates, the merchant group that, all you gentlemen know, was in charge of this entire colony and all its trade until this 'last' year, when the king took over. Such associations are rarely seen in Spain, because the Spanish manage their overseas settlements through their monarchies, not their merchants. But such associations have always been in England, much to our chagrin, most prominently the East India Company. In summary, merchants are the fourth source of the power heretofore mentioned in the first stanza."

Philippe's chair scraped as he pushed himself away from the table. No longer a mask, his face was a scowl. His knuckles, pressed against his knee, whitened.

Moments ago, during the card game, she had feared Philippe and Louis-Jacques might come to blows in their rivalry. Though she disapproved of any violence, she could not deny the wickedly powerful thrill she'd experienced at the thought of these two brawny men mentally fencing over her. After her mother died and Marietta came of age, and before her father had been pushed out of his position, her father had always brought her along with him to the many diplomatic affairs and social events, so she was not unfamiliar with the way men vied for a woman's attention, but there was something deeper and far more gripping in the rivalry between these two men. Perhaps because, this time, without doubt, in this strange place and situation, one of them was likely to become her husband.

A partner for life.

"And so we come to the final stanza,"

Louis-Jacques announced. "Which brings the first four stanzas together. It says '*my whole from Jupiter's court on high,*' for which again I must congratulate our Marietta, who knows enough of Roman myths to understand that Jupiter is the king of all the lesser gods, Zeus in Greek mythology. To all of us, who else could this refer to but our most beloved King Louis? It is he who '*descends to cheer the whole earth,*' and '*without whose presence, there would be of happiness a dearth.*'"

Her mind was racing but she froze her smile as Louis-Jacques continued in his folly.

What else could she do?

"And so," he added, dropping his voice a fraction, "the answer to Marietta's riddle—which speaks of the combined power of princes and priests and merchants, can refer only to our beloved France and its glorious monarchy, which recently in fatherly love has chosen to administer this new settlement."

A moment of silence fell upon the room, but for the crackling of the logs in the hearth fire, a silence so painful, Marietta felt as if it pierced her ears. Around the six tables, chins puckered, beards were stroked, and heads began to nod. Madame Bourdon had arrived sometime during the recitation, and now she stood in the parlor doorway, breath bated, watching Marietta as she clutched her hands against her chest. Though Marietta couldn't bring herself to look down, she felt Philippe's piercing perusal like twin spots of fire upon her face.

The path was free between where she stood and the doorway that led out of the parlor, she noticed. Physically, she could dart out at any time, but, really, only diplomacy could release her from this dilemma.

"Monsieur Blanchet." She had to force out the words, her throat flexed so sore. "How you flatter me, sir, with your many compliments."

"Not idly or without reason." He watched her face with the intensity of a hawk fixed on the wriggling of a mouse. "I feel no shame in confessing that I stole many hours from my duties during the effort to solve your riddle."

"Yours," she began, feeling like she was running out of breath, "is a wise and well-thought-out solution."

"And you have paid a fine compliment to our king in composing it."

"Your unraveling is clever." Could she do this? She'd set the rules. How could she break, or even bend them, without marring her own character? And why was she hesitating anyway, when the man fit every expectation?

"In fact, sir." She braced herself. "Your solution is clever enough that I must fulfill my promise. I invite you to court me, if that is your pleasure."

"Miss Marietta." Louis-Jacques's face split in that grin again, the one that made him look less a great dignitary and more like an eager boy. "There is nothing I desire more."

A collective sigh went up in the room, along with a few groans from the men. Madame Bourdon leapt a little where she stood in the parlor portal. Polite applause ensued, and Louis-Jacques had the presence of mind to bow to each corner of the room. Her suitor would feast on this victory, she thought, at every dinner he attended. She could almost see his chest puffing out, stretching the costly brass buttons and their triply sewn buttonholes.

Philippe, however, had collapsed back against his chair as if propelled by the singing shaft of an iron-tipped arrow, his face a rictus of dismay.

"However," she added, her heart squeezing, "your solution puts me in a dilemma, sir." Damn her tongue, what was she doing? Just because her heart was torn didn't mean she shouldn't listen to her wiser self. "There is just one modification to my promise that I am compelled, by honor, to add."

Louis-Jacques did not look pleased, but perversely, that only made the words surge faster to her lips.

"The solution you offer," she said, "is so very well constructed that I accept it, and I'm very willing and grateful to do so. My promise stands, and will stand, even after what I'm about to say."

"Miss Marietta," Louis-Jacques murmured, "please, no more riddles."

"Your solution is brilliant…but it is not

the solution for which this riddle was composed."

Amid a collective gasp, she met Louis-Jacques's steady gaze, waiting to see how he would react to the news, testing him a little, though she felt wicked for doing so.

Louis-Jacques, to his credit, made no objection.

She continued, "Riddles often have several solutions, for those clever enough to think them up, like you have, but the true solution to this riddle is far, far simpler than the one you have offered." She pressed a hand against her stomach to stop its roiling. "And so I feel bound to continue to honor my original promise to the men of Quebec, and allow others to offer solutions until the true answer is revealed."

Gasps went up amid the crowd. Madame Bourdon shook her head. Marietta didn't look at Philippe—compelled to keep her chin up, her resolve steady—but she glimpsed from the corner of her eye a sly smile tugging the scar of his face.

"You are a woman of great honor, Miss

Marietta." Louis-Jacques tilted his head and offered her another bow. "Of course the real answer must be revealed. I suspect I'm about to steal more hours from my duties to think up a simpler solution, for I am curious as to what that solution is myself."

"Thank you, sir." She let go of the breath she hadn't realized she'd been holding. "Your graciousness reflects well upon your character."

"And your dedication to fairness does the same for you." Louis-Jacques turned toward Madame Bourdon. "Now, shall we pull the corks from those bottles I brought, Madame Bourdon? I'd like to make a toast to my darling Marietta, always so full of surprises."

CHAPTER TEN

The next day, walking up the cliffside hill from the lower town to the upper, Philippe stopped in his muddy tracks just as they rounded a curve.

Marietta stood some ways up the slope, in front of a merchant's shop whose door was draped in pine garlands.

His heart lifted. By candlelight, by firelight, or in the dull gray light of a winter afternoon, Marietta in his eyes was perpetually surrounded by her own light.

Then Philippe's gaze slid to her companion, and as quickly as his heart had lifted, it dropped to his feet. She was accompanied by that wretched Louis-of-a-dozen-names Blanchet, her new suitor, the man who'd won so much more than a card game yesterday.

"Now, Philippe," André said, laying a heavy hand on his arm. "The last time I saw that look on your face, we found ourselves in a brawl."

"I won't fight the man."

Though he wanted to, in a deep, dark part of himself. His fists itched to bruise the man's good looks and dirty his fine clothes, thus proving himself the stronger, hardier, and better fighter. But he knew that would only make Marietta furious and extinguish any hope he had of winning her heart.

Yes, her heart.

As mad as that seemed, it was what he wanted.

He could deny it no longer.

Andre's grip on Philippe's arm tightened. "Listen to reason, my friend."

Why start now?

"Blanchet won the right to court her fairly," André argued. "He answered the riddle, and she has allowed him—"

"To court," Philippe interrupted, "not necessarily to marry."

"There's little difference around here, you know that. One follows quickly after the other."

"Maybe not this time." Philippe watched as Marietta, standing in front of the merchant's doorway, rifled through boxes, tied with twine that Louis-of-a-dozen-names held piled up in his arms. She wasn't looking at the man, wasn't smiling up at him or laughing or blushing or even *talking,* and that gave him some ease. She was treating Blanchet as nothing more than a porter, though Philippe wondered if that was just his hopes talking.

"I've been thinking," Philippe murmured, half to André, half to himself. "I just need to find a way—"

"A way to do what?" André dropped his grip on Philippe's arm and sighed. "She's here to be married, and you're here to help me make this exploration voyage happen, for both of us. If we can just secure the funding from the bishop today, our future will be set.

Forget her, Philippe. Move along and think about our plans."

Philippe nodded, more out of habit than conviction. Yesterday at the card party, his world had exploded, in a way not unlike the time he'd seen a spark from a torch fall upon a keg of black powder on a ship moored in Dieppe, splitting the night with a crack and a billow of foul-smelling smoke. On that day, the world had been obscured for hours…and, in the case of yesterday, the smoke in his brain had not yet fully cleared. He still couldn't quite believe he'd witnessed Marietta offering her favors to the wrong man yesterday, the man of a dozen names.

But there she was now, escorted by that ass, who stood irritatingly close to her.

As if he had a right to.

"We're going to walk now, Philippe. We've got places to go." André nudged him with his shoulder. "It's best to arrive early at the bishop's. As we pass Miss Marietta and your rival, you're going to say a polite hello, acknowledge both of them with a nod, and just keep walking."

His feet moved. Bits of muddy gravel rolled under the bottom of his boots, but his legs were leaden. Last night, fortified by a goodly amount of rum, he'd fallen asleep praying a new dream would reveal some wisdom, but instead, he dreamt the other two dreams yet again. The stag wandering in the deep woods in search of moonlight on a flower, followed by the vision of his dirty, work-hardened hands laying stone upon stone. He'd begun to wonder if those visions were really meant to lead him to André and his voyage, since they still persisted though he was already committed… His shock-and-rum-muddled mind struggled to remember why he'd been so sure of that conclusion, and, with the elders of his Abenaki people hundreds of miles away, hunting the winter fields and forests on the other side of the St. Lawrence River, Philippe had no one to share his visions with and feared he might never be able to discern the true meaning.

As he and André approached the shop and the distracted couple, Marietta still fussing with the boxes, a boy came running down the slope. A missive in his hand flapped in the breeze of his barely controlled headlong charge. The boy skidded to a stop beside Blanchet, giving Philippe a measure of childish pleasure as the boy unwittingly kicked slush and mud onto Blanchet's fine-leather, turned-over boots.

Marietta stopped fussing with the boxes and frowned at the interruption. Philippe heard the boy's high-pitched voice, but not the words he spoke to Blanchet. The boy, still breathless, unfolded the paper and lifted it so Louis-of-a-dozen-names could read it over the top of the pile of boxes in his arms.

Philippe stopped in his tracks for the second time, as Louis-of-a-dozen-names glanced about the busy street, ceasing only when Blanchet's gaze locked with his own.

André cursed under his breath, but Philippe straightened in response to Blanchet's furious frown. The ass's expression all but accused Philippe of stalking them. He wasn't, although the thought had passed his mind. He was here by coincidence no matter what Blanchet chose to think. The streets of the settlement were public spaces, free for all of them to walk, and this mountain cliff path was the busiest of them, since this curving slope path was the only one that connected the lower town with the upper one.

She is not your wife yet.

Blanchet shifted his gaze to the people walking about the hillside, but then returned, reluctantly, to him. "Monsieur Martineau," the ass shouted. "Might I have a word?"

Philippe said, "Of course," and slid a glance to Marietta, whose face, framed by a fox-fur-lined hood, had gone unusually pale.

"Stop staring at her," André said under his breath as they walked toward the couple. "He's as aware of your attraction to that woman as I am, but he doesn't have your best interests in mind, Philippe. Don't let him bait you."

"Monsieur Martineau," Louis-of-a-dozen-names said, bowing his head in greeting. "What a coincidence to find you here."

"We're off to see Bishop Laval for business," André offered before Philippe could speak. André held out his hand before dropping it when realizing Blanchet's hands were full of boxes, and so he couldn't shake. "I am André Lefebvre, a friend of Monsieur Martineau, at your service."

Blanchet said, with reluctance in his voice, "It is Monsieur Martineau's service I am hoping for."

How interesting. "What can I do for you, Blanchet?" *Other than steal away the woman you're courting?*

"I've been summoned to the governor's house on an urgent matter." He tilted his head to the page, standing a little bit away, still trying to catch his breath. "But as Miss Marietta's escort, I cannot leave her unattended. Nor do I have the time to bring her back to Madame Bourdon's."

Philippe's heart leapt. "I'd be more than happy"—*to take your place*—"to see her safely home."

The lift of Blanchet's brow suggested he knew exactly how happy Philippe was for the opportunity.

"Of course," Blanchet said, turning to Marietta, "I make the offer only with

Marietta's permission."

"Louis, I have no objection." She placed a hand on his arm. "Such important work can't wait. I'm content to have Monsieur Martineau and his friend—Monsieur Lefebvre?—bring me home."

Philippe's gut tightened at the sight of her glove on Blanchet's arm, but she removed it swiftly enough when Blanchet approached and slid the pile of packages into Philippe's arms. The packages weren't particularly heavy, but they were bulky and had a tendency to slide, and Philippe had to lean sideways to see beyond them.

"Many thanks, sir," Blanchet said with a dark warning in his voice, before stepping away, bowing over Marietta's hand and heading up the slope, trailing the boy.

Philippe promptly turned to André and offered him the packages. At first surprised, balking, André finally sighed and shook his head as he took on the burden. The flash of André's rum-colored eyes suggested Philippe would be paying the tavern bill tonight.

Philippe didn't care. Thoughts of taverns

and packages and André left his mind the minute he turned and offered Marietta his arm.

Her deep, dark brown eyes swam with suspicion as she curled her gloved hand under his elbow. "How very convenient that you happened to be around, sir, when that messenger came."

"Luck, Miss Marietta." He drew her close by tucking his arm against his side. "Pure luck. You heard André. We are on the way to a business meeting. And what brings you here?"

"Shopping. Of course." She glanced over her shoulder, presumably at André following dutifully, packages in his arms. "Madame Bourdon gave me an allowance to buy gifts for the children for New Year's Day."

"Were you successful?"

"Obviously." How he loved how her brow puckered when she was deep in thought. "But only in part. I had hoped to get something for Madame Bourdon too, fabrics or some little luxury, perfume, or a scented soap, but the merchants don't have much to offer."

"Most folks will have bought their New Year's gifts early, long before the last ships left, knowing that no other luxuries would be coming to these shores again, not until June."

"It's odd to be cut off from the rest of the world for so many months of the year." She shrugged. He felt the movement of her shoulder against his own. "Fortunately, the local woodworkers have delightful painted tops and games and dolls for the children, so the young ones will not feel the lack. Be honest with me, Philippe. Was it really due to luck that you found yourself here, or did you arrange this whole little sly distraction?"

"Pure luck." He leaned close enough to feel a lock of her hair, flying loose of her hood, against his jaw. "Now be honest with me. Do you have any rule against courting two men?"

She tsked and turned her head to face him. "You haven't earned the privilege, sir."

"Nearly drowning doesn't count?"

"Don't rewrite history. I warned you *not* to race. You got yourself in that situation." She sighed, returning her attention to the steepest part of the slope. "Besides, *he* solved the riddle—"

"Not correctly."

"Nonetheless, his reasoning was sound. What kind of woman would I be if I denied him after all his extreme efforts?"

"Do you love him?"

He couldn't believe he'd said that, and by the way her face flushed, neither did she, but there it was.

Marietta yanked her hand from under his elbow. "What kind of question is that?"

"An honest one."

"Courtship…marriage… There are many factors a woman must consider when her future is at stake, and love is only one of them."

"That's a no, then?"

"I did not say that. I hardly know him well enough to…" She huffed out a sigh. "This is not about *him*. This is about you and me, Monsieur Philippe. We want very different things, I think."

"We hardly know each other. If you would see it in your heart to loosen your rules and allow me to court you—"

"Are you not committed to a voyage to the west come fall?"

His jaw tightened. He looked far ahead of him, toward the upper city, coming into view, but he saw no path away from that truth.

She persisted, "Are you not currently, right this moment, on the way to a meeting to secure funding for that very voyage?"

"Right now," Philippe hedged, "I'm taking a detour in order to escort you back to Madame Bourdon."

André made a sound behind them, but it was muffled with distance, and perhaps because he spoke into a pile of boxes.

"Sir, in my life, I have known great comfort, and I have known great poverty."

Surprise kept him mute. What was this about?

She added, "Also, I have known the joy of family, and I have known the pains of absolute solitude."

So have I.

He held the words and his breath.

"Because of those experiences, I know

what I want for my future. In this I am resolved." She hugged her arms, the leather of her gloves digging into the sleeves of her coat. "I hope for some measure of comfort, of course. A woman would be a fool not to. Marriage defines our entire future. But more than comfort, *much* more than that, I crave the constant companionship of a kind husband who understands the value of setting down roots and building a home and family—and now I've said too much."

With more speed than he thought possible, Marietta darted ahead of him, laboring on the slope until she reached a more level area, where she lengthened her stride and quickened her pace even more. He followed at a distance, but did not try to catch up, his thoughts in a whirl.

"You promised to *escort* her," André muttered as he passed Philippe with his armful of packages, following Marietta's twitching skirts. "What is wrong with you? One minute, you can't keep your eyes off her, and the next, you're letting her go."

André didn't wait for an answer, just

hurried to keep up with Marietta. Which was fine, because Philippe didn't really have an answer for his behavior, except that what she'd just revealed about her own life had dazed him. So he watched as André overtook her only a few steps away from the door to Madame Bourdon's home. There, Marietta turned to André and dipped in a graceful curtsy, and the door swung open, and Madame Bourdon invited André in, taking the boxes in hand. But once released of his burdens, André took a step away from the door and bowed and shook his head and pointed back to where Philippe, still in a stupor, stood in the middle of the dirty road and tried to make sense of what Marietta had just revealed.

Everything began to make sense.

He'd never examined his life in the same way she did, but now he couldn't help but draw a connection between their families, their early lives. His family had had many years when they were comfortable, when the fish were running and his father had many good hauls and people were eager to buy his catch. Those were the easiest of his childhood years. Even after his mother died, and then his brother, he and his father still had comfort but no joy, for the losses lingered. But once his father had succumbed to a fever and Philippe had been left alone, he'd learned how to survive the lack of comfort in the port of Dieppe, but he'd never shaken the pain of solitude. Running away from the place and the pain, he'd taken a ship to these settlements, where one of the first things he'd done was find a new family, unexpected but so deeply longed for, among the Abenaki.

Now he realized that Marietta had had a similar lived experience. A comfortable upbringing, a loss of a parent, then the loss of the other, followed by an urge to leave home. The difference was this: Marietta knew what she wanted, what she needed. Perhaps, like her, what he was really searching for was that old familiar mix of comfort and joy.

"Philippe."

André stepped in front of Philippe, arms akimbo, waiting until Philippe gave him his full attention before speaking again.

"Put this matter of Miss Marietta behind you," André said, "and concentrate on the meeting with the bishop. Our voyage will not happen without your tremendous powers of persuasion."

Philippe only half heard what André was saying. For André, nothing had changed. His friend's focus remained solely on the funding and arrangements for the voyage to the west. But Philippe's whole world had turned upside down. He could no longer shake the conviction that it was his duty as well as his destiny to give Marietta—and himself—everything they both wanted.

"André." Philippe slapped a hand on his friend's broad shoulder. "Indulge me while I propose a change of plans…"

CHAPTER ELEVEN

"Monsieur Blanchet," Marietta said, looking up at him from the pillow of her skirts. She sat on the floor of Madame Bourdon's foyer, wrestling a fur-lined boot onto the foot of one of the younger children, while Louis stood beside her. "I can't thank you enough for agreeing to join us on this excursion."

Louis nodded from his great height. He hadn't yet shed his outdoor clothes since arriving moments ago. He looked dumbfounded at the number of children squirming at his feet, struggling into their boots and gloves and hats and coats with some help and gentle scolding from her and

Isabelle.

"With New Year's coming just the day after tomorrow, Madame Bourdon has *so* much to do," Marietta persisted, feeling obliged to press her case, for she'd had to coax Louis into agreeing to accompany them to the ice slide that everyone was talking about, dug into one of the slopes of the upper town. She knew her polite beau had hoped to spend the day with her alone, and now here they were in the company of half a dozen children. She felt a little guilty at the ruse. "Madame works so hard to present a sumptuous réveillon for New Year's, and the best way to aid her is to take the children out on an excursion like this so she'll have an hour or two of peace. You will be coming, won't you? To the réveillon?"

Louis focused on her for a moment. "I wouldn't miss an opportunity to sit at your side, Miss Marietta."

"Oh." She should be thrilled. Louis was a wonderful storyteller, an amusing companion, and a handsome man. "I thought the governor might insist you attend his festivities," she said. "I know he is serving up his own feast, and he is so often in need of your skills."

"I've spoken to the governor about this matter." Louis's smile stretched, a smile that probably held secrets but she couldn't read them clearly enough. "I'll attend his feast for the main course, but come here for Madame Bourdon's legendary sweets. The governor has agreed to this. He understands where my intentions lie."

She couldn't mistake his intentions, and though she admired his certainty, she hadn't yet found that same certainty in herself. So she chose to avoid comment and instead glanced down at Raoul, barely four, who'd flopped on his back as she struggled to shove his foot into the other boot. The boots seemed a touch snug. Children's feet grew so fast, and yet these boots were bought only a few days ago, after the skating excursion with Philippe.

Her cheeks grew warm. There he was again, coming to mind, when she should be thinking of other matters. Why was Philippe always in her head? She was still so ashamed of herself after her runaway mouth yesterday, when Philippe had escorted her partway home.

The boot in her hand filled with Raoul's foot, and the boy popped up to toddle about, rotund in his coat.

"Very well." She stood from the pool of her skirts. "I think we're all ready." All but the baby, who was too young to attend, and little Marie, who had woken up cranky and sniffling.

She reached for her own coat, the last one hanging on the pegs. Louis gallantly set his ornamental cane aside to help her into it, and she bent her head forward so his fingers wouldn't brush her bare neck, for she'd tucked her hair up into a fur hat.

To ease the sting of that gentle rebuff, she laid her gloved hand on his arm.

"Come, children," she said, following Louis-Jacques out of the house and into the bracing cold. "The slide awaits."

Yesterday, when Louis had accompanied her to several merchant's shops—remarkably patient and attentive—she'd glimpsed the ice slide carved upon a hilly section of the upper town. Seeing all the adults and children swarming around it, she was determined to find a way to bring the Bourdon children there so all the business at the house wouldn't result in them missing out on the winter entertainment the settlement had to offer. She knew she had surprised Louis this morning and put him off a bit, because she'd told him yesterday that she would be spending today embroidering doll dresses and he was welcome to sit by the fire with her as she worked her needle. But life in a busy household required swift adaptation. She had an obligation to be a good helper to Madame Bourdon, and also a true desire to make the twelve days of Christmas magical for the children, in a way that it had been when her father was alive, for she remembered their Christmases in so many countries, adapting to new traditions everywhere they went. She held those memories dear.

Her new beau would have to adapt.

Sliding a gaze toward him across the

heads of the chattering children, she noticed that he seemed to have shaken off his earlier disappointment. He swung his cane, spearing it into the icy ground, walking with a little more spring in his step, his chin high as he nodded to acquaintances they passed on the way.

Well done, Louis.

If only Louis would talk to the children too, engage with them in some kind way.

Never mind that, she told herself, shaking off the thought. Just because Philippe knew how to tease a child, to be playful enough to toss a young boy his hat or pinch his cheek or ask a twelve-year-old boy questions to bring him into the conversation…well, there was more to any man than an ease with children, and she suspected that quality could be learned once a man had children of his own.

The children gasped as the ice slide came into view. Unlike the lower town, which was flat and featureless from the river's lapping edge to the sudden thrust of the quartz-encrusted escarpment called Cap Diamant, the upper town where Madame Bourdon and the children lived had many uneven, hilly features. The makers of the slide had taken advantage of the area's natural hill to carve a chute with snowy walls that began at the top and then curved around to spit out the sliders at the bottom. Marietta's gut twisted as she witnessed some older boys flying out of the base of the slide's chute so quickly that they tumbled and rolled and ultimately slammed into the packed snow wall that acted as a stop. They laughed and popped up unharmed in the way young boys often did, but she worried if the slide was too dangerous for the younger children.

She glanced toward Louis, hoping he might catch her eye and see her dismay and offer to accompany the younger children on the slide, but Louis's gaze continued to run over the crowd as if in search of more acquaintances. As Louis *would* do, she realized, thinking of yesterday's jaunt to the shops, when her suitor had had a conversation with every merchant in the stores, and every shopper both inside and out. Louis was an ambitious man who took great pains to cultivate his social circle, a venture that, as a diplomat's daughter, she heartily understood.

And approved of, of course.

Ambition was attractive in a man.

But right now…she had more immediate concerns.

Jean-Baptiste soon lost patience with the delay. He broke from the huddle with his siblings and bolted toward the slide. She didn't have the heart to insist he stop and wait for his brothers and sisters. As the oldest of the family, much was expected of Jean-Baptiste, but Marietta felt that a boy of high spirits and much responsibility deserved to go off on his own every once in a while. Perhaps if he did a few rounds on the ride, he'd work off the novelty and the excitement, and then when she drafted him into service to his younger siblings, he would be more willing to take the role of a mentor.

Besides, she had no fears for Jean-Baptiste on the slide. A boy that young knew how to bounce rather than break.

She sidled up to Louis and spoke in low tones. "I'll take Raoul on my lap first, to see how scary the slide might be for the younger ones."

Louis nodded absently, still squinting against the sunlight glancing off the snow and ice. "I'll watch these others until you emerge."

That wasn't the answer she'd hoped for. Indeed, Louis, in his fine woolen cloak with its brass buttons, might look a little silly sliding in the middle of the day, fine French boots flying up, even with a child on his lap. But…still. She'd hoped for a little participation on his part.

She sighed, anticipating an exhausting afternoon. Perhaps she should have worked harder to convince Isabelle to join them, for even Isabelle in her cautious frailty would have seen the necessity of pitching in.

"Children, you wait here with Monsieur Blanchet." Two of the older ones looked frustrated, but the younger two looked relieved, transfixed with wide eyes by the chaotic way many of the children rolled out of the slide, some on their bellies, others backward. "When I return," she said with a glance at her distracted beau, "we'll figure out a way to pair up."

Hauling Raoul upon her hip, she trudged up the hill, breathing hard by the time she reached the line at the top. She picked out one of the larger deerskin "sleds" from a pile. A man who looked remarkably like Gaspard from the ice-skating venture—but who only greeted her with a smile—instructed her on where to set down the hide on the greased side, while warning her to keep her skirts and arms folded close as they made the trip down.

Raoul wriggled in her arms, but she didn't put him down until it was time for her to sit on the deerskin and then take him firmly onto her lap. She nestled his fur-padded body between her thighs and crossed her ankles so he was wedged and secure. A pulse pounded in her ears as she stared down at the blue-white ice and the snow walls that rose up on either side, nearly making a tunnel. Sitting as she was, she could barely see over either side. Just ahead, over the wall that covered a lower curve of the slide farther down, she glimpsed the grand vista that made the upper town such an elegant place to live, the view of the wide St. Lawrence River. She wondered if the hill was chosen for the construction of the slide because it was one of the highest points on the upper town. It certainly seemed that way by the angle of the vista. But she didn't have time to enjoy the familiar view, for the man who must be Gaspard's twin planted a hand on her back and gave her a push and then—and then—she was flying!

On her lap, Raoul squealed in glee as the ice slope dropped below them. The sudden swoop threatened to push her legs over her head, but she forced herself to lean forward and resist that force. The chill bit her cheeks and funneled through the lock of hair that had escaped her hat. A swift curve sent the deerskin sliding up one side of the snowy wall, and then another curve sent it sliding slightly up the other. Raoul giggled and raised his arms, stubby in the fur-lined sleeves. The giggle filled her heart, and then she realized she was laughing too as the ice continued to slope down and she slid along at a delightful speed, and before she could quite catch her breath, they shot out of the end of the slide, approached a break wall of snow, the rougher, softer surface now beneath their deerskin acting as a brake as they eased to a stop just a few feet before the snow pack.

Raoul hurled himself off her skirts and, staggering, pointed to the top of the slide.

"Again! Again!"

"Yes," she said, scrambling up before the people now emerging from the slide swept her off her feet. She tossed the deerskin on a wooden sled swiftly filling with other discarded skins, before seizing Raoul's hand and steering him out of danger and toward his siblings. "But first, your sisters and brothers will want a turn."

Trudging through the snow, paying more attention to where she put her boots and lifting little Raoul up when the bootstep ridges proved too deep for him, Marietta didn't notice the man who had joined Louis and their little party until she was nearly upon them all.

The stranger turned his head at her approach, and she recognized him as the woods runner who had carried her packages yesterday. Philippe's good friend André.

"Why, hello, Monsieur Lefebvre." She bowed her head, unable to keep the surprise out of her voice. "What a strange coincidence to see you here."

"I was passing by and saw many friends and acquaintances gathered. I couldn't resist watching for a moment."

She nodded as if listening, but she was really looking for Philippe. He had to be close, for these two men were inseparable. She assumed Philippe knew she would come here today—though that made no sense, since she'd only just made the decision this morning. And hadn't she been thinking about the possibility of bumping into him again since the very moment she decided it was a good day to bring the children on an excursion? And yet, looking and looking around the whole crowd, she saw no sign of him.

Disappointment dove deep.

Had she put him off altogether yesterday?

Wasn't that what she'd wanted to do?

Against her better judgment, she heard

herself saying to André, "Where is your business partner today, sir? I rarely see you without him."

"He has…a new project he's working on."

"Indeed?"

"Yes." André flashed a smile. A little too knowing, in her opinion. "Philippe is a brilliant business partner, but sometimes he insists on carving his own path."

Curiosity nibbled at her, but she would just make things worse by asking, for Louis's discomfort with the conversation was obvious. Raoul saved her from herself as he began wriggling anew in her arms, pointing toward the slide, making "wanting" noises, yelling, "Again, again," a song that the other children joined in, in a terrible cacophony.

"You certainly have your hands full today," André remarked as his gaze fell upon Raoul with a softness that was startling upon such a weathered face. "This tot, he's about the age of…" André shook his head, and then held out his arms. "With your permission, miss, I could take this eager one for a ride down the slide and save you to take care of the many others. I promise, I'll treat him like glass, I assure you."

"I have no worries," she conceded, handing Raoul over, for the boy was already stretching his arms toward André. "Raoul is a little young, he doesn't quite have the sense to stay still on the deerskin yet. I wouldn't trust him on the slide alone, so yes, sir, I very much appreciate your offer."

"My pleasure. Come here, you." André took the boy and hauled him over his shoulder like a pack of furs, to Raoul's giddy delight, and then André stomped up the hill, balancing the boy with one strong arm, as she imagined any woods runner might do with a cask or packet during a portage around river rapids.

Turning back to Louis, Marietta saw how her beau squinted after André before glancing down at the five children remaining as if seeing them for the first time and realizing he had certain obligations. She stayed silent for one short but significant moment. Silence could be very powerful, Marietta knew, but even more powerful was the manly urge not to be outdone by another man in the presence of an available woman.

Louis muttered, "I grew up in Poitiers. I've never been on an ice slide."

"It's utterly delightful," she said, encouraging him. "It feels like flying."

"Hmmm." Louis frowned at the children, who were jumping up and down like rabbits beside him. "I suppose I could give it a try, take one or two of these enthusiastic Bourdons with me."

Enthusiastic Bourdons. As if they were interchangeable. *Don't be petty.* "Thank you, Louis, that would be a great relief."

"Anything for you, darling Marietta."

With a wink, Louis walked toward a tree a short distance away to lean his cane upon it. Marietta turned to the two older girls and tilted her head toward the slide. "You two have my permission to go on the slide either alone or together, as you wish."

They nodded and bolted away. Marietta watched as they kicked up their skirts, running in the wake of André and their youngest brother. Then she turned her attention to the three children that remained. Louis, coming back, took the hands of the two younger boys, who were already holding them out to him. With a sigh, Louis glanced up the slope, shrugged, and headed off, shoulders forward.

He was a dignified man, she told herself. Would the governor ever come here and hurl himself down an ice slide? No, he wouldn't. He would think the activity was beneath him, and probably beneath the members of his council too, like Louis. All the more reason why Louis should be commended for taking up such childish doings. Didn't his willingness to throw himself into an activity that made him uneasy speak well of his admiration for her, of his ability to compromise, and his keenness to win her affections?

Yes.

And yet…and yet…

"Come on, Helene." Marietta took Helene's hand, the lone Bourdon child left, the oft-forgotten middle child, and then followed the others at a slower pace.

"You don't have to go with me, Miss

Marietta," she said. "Last year, I slid down the slide all by myself."

"Did you? I didn't know that." Marietta loosened her grip, allowing the girl to drop her hand if she chose. "In that case, you have my permission to head up on your own."

"Well, I can do it myself…if I *want* to." Helene clung more tightly to Marietta's hand. "Sometimes I change my mind."

Marietta smiled. Helene, barely nine, was awfully young to realize that sometimes she didn't have to follow rules…but, as a middle child, her needs were so often left unmet—or left for last—as the adults took care of the older and younger siblings, that Marietta couldn't help but notice that Helene had too often been left to her own devices.

"So," Marietta ventured, determined to nurture the girl's wisdom to make good decisions, "are you saying that you would like me to join you?"

"I don't know." Helene's face had paled, despite the bright spots of pink on her cheeks from the cold. She was clearly frightened by the slide. "I'll decide when I get to the top.

I'm still thinking about it. I don't know what I want right now."

"I see." Marietta glanced up at her beau's broad back as he preceded her up the slope. "I understand how it feels not to know what is best, Helene. I understand…completely."

CHAPTER TWELVE

The tavern was so full of drunken men this New Year's Eve that Philippe, sitting in the farthest corner of the dim room, could barely hear his own thoughts.

He needed to hear his thoughts if he was ever going to solve Marietta's riddle.

Gritting his teeth as a clutch of men started singing another canoeing song, he leaned over the wax slate in his hand, squinting in the dim candlelight at the scratches he'd made with the point of his knife, considering how much longer he could puzzle things out under these conditions, with the smell of spilled rum in his nostrils and the revelry deafening him. But his options concerning Marietta had dwindled to one, and so, since persuasion and charm hadn't worked, he was determined to unlock Marietta's puzzle. He'd spent all but one hour of the last twenty-four locked in his room upstairs, the tiny garret he shared with André, until the walls had begun to close in on him.

Concentrate.

It can't be this hard.

He raised his head to glare anew at the wall beside him, where the twenty lines of the riddle were scrawled in fading ash. This puzzle was impossible, as impossible to understand as the woman he loved beyond reason.

He twitched at the unfamiliar word *love*, but knew it was true.

He was convinced.

Philippe startled at the noise of a tin cup slamming on wood. It was a common sound in this place—except this time the sound happened close, and the impact shook the table. He glanced at the rum sloshing out of the cup that appeared at his elbow, and then up at the tall, grinning devil who'd put it down hard enough to grab his attention.

Philippe sighed and nudged the cup away. "Not now, André."

"*Yes,* now." André nudged the cup back. "It's New Year's Eve, my friend. Everyone here is celebrating but you. You're sitting here brooding."

"I'm working."

"No one should work on New Year's Eve."

"Except tavern keepers and their families," he remarked, jerking a chin at the innkeeper behind a small bar, who'd brought in his wife and sons to help keep the rum flowing during this raucous, spontaneous réveillon of lost souls. "Do you know who also works on New Year's Eve?" He ruefully raised his slate. "Me and other lovesick fools."

"At least you admit it."

"I will win her heart. It's her I seek—"

"According to your dreams, I know."

Philippe's jaw hardened, for he'd hoped this matter would not fester between him and his friend. When he'd first come upon André many months ago and heard André's plans for a voyage west, Philippe had sincerely believed his dreams aligned with André's plans, and so he'd joined him. Some months later, when difficulties prevented their voyage from going forward, and when André was on the verge of giving up his goals altogether, Philippe had confessed the stuff of his nightly visions so that André would understand that his friend's grand plans to *seek* had been foretold. Since André spoke Huron and knew many of the ways of the Huron and Abenaki, his friend had listened with respect to Philippe's dreams, and, thus inspired, took up his plans with renewed fervor, just as Philippe had intended. But now…now that Philippe understood his dreams in a different way—and knew that he himself was the stag wandering in the dark woods, and the moon flower he sought was Marietta, and that the vision of piling stone upon stone was a vision of building a different kind of future from what André was planning…he supposed André couldn't help but be disappointed, even if Philippe had promised not to abandon the venture, but just take on a different role.

Then he remembered some news about

that new role that might cheer André out of his scowl. "I spoke to Monsieur Bourdon yesterday."

"About scolding your lovely Marietta to have done with this riddle nonsense?"

"Of course not. Marietta wasn't even at home."

Much to his chagrin.

"I know exactly where she was yesterday." André all but collapsed into the seat across from Philippe and set his elbows on the sticky table. "I saw her at the ice slide with Monsieur Oh-So-Fashionable. They were there with a great number of Bourdon children, including that little pip, Raoul."

"Of course." What happened to his intuition? He should have wandered over to the ice slide after he'd visited Monsieur Bourdon yesterday, during the brief hour he'd left his room. Of course she would bring the children there on such a fine day, but what could he have said to her anyway, when his new plans were yet unfinished and she'd told him just the day before that she didn't think they were compatible?

The subject frustrated him, so he shifted it back again. "What matters, André, and what you'll be interested to hear is that when I visited Monsieur Bourdon, he was enthusiastic about the chance to help fund the building of another warehouse in the lower town. He's eager to make some serious competition for old Antoine."

"Smart man, Bourdon." André wiggled his near-empty cup toward the tavern keeper, a signal for more. "I'm amazed, though. I thought we'd tapped that source of funds dry."

"Apparently not. Though Bourdon didn't offer to be the sole investor. He talked about encouraging several partners to join. He said he would make inquiries for me."

"Well done. You could sell furs to a bear, Philippe."

"Exactly. You need to remember that and not be so sour with me. My new plans will help you," Philippe insisted. "If I stay in Quebec, then while you're off exploring you'll have a man you trust guarding your trading goods and also taking care of all the rules and regulations and political nonsense we've been dealing with these past months, which is only going to get worse—"

"Yes, yes, you've made your case." André lifted his cup as the shadow of the tavern keeper's son fell over them and the boy poured more rum into it. "But I'm still angry about your decision because I value your good company, my friend, more than I do many of these fools, especially in the wilderness." As the boy went to another table, André gestured with his sloshing cup to the men in the tavern, several of whom, like the Rossier brothers and Wapishka, had already committed to the voyage. "And yet I find it in my heart to forgive you, Philippe, because you're in love."

Yes.

His heart swelled.

Yes.

"I recently had a reason to remember what that means." André gazed beyond Philippe's right shoulder, beyond the walls of the tavern, to some distant spot unseen. "Yesterday, I held a boy in my arms who is the same age that my child would have been had Rose lived to give birth. Holding him reminded me of…so much lost."

Philippe held his tongue. André spoke so seldom about the loss of his wife and child that Philippe was loath to interrupt.

"Frankly," André continued, "all those years ago, I should have piled stone upon stone to build Rose a safe place to live here in the settlement, behind palisade walls." André's gaze refocused on him with sudden intensity. "As you now wish to do for Marietta."

"Let's hope I have the opportunity." Philippe acquiesced to the warning in André's eyes to change the subject, and so he waved his fingers at the words on the wall beside them. "I can't even think about building a home until I solve this wretched thing and win the right to court her."

"You've been working on that like a monk, and from what I can tell by the scratches on that tablet, you don't seem any closer to solving it." André nudged Philippe's untouched tin cup a little closer to him. "Maybe a distraction and a little rum will bring inspiration."

"You're the devil. Stop tempting me."

"I'm on your side, old friend. I *want* you to solve it. Sooner rather than later, though."

"Rum will not help."

"It may, after I finish telling you something." André sighed and ran his fingers through his long, unruly hair. "I've got some bad news, my friend. About Marietta's suitor, Blanchet."

Philippe's stomach clenched.

André said, "I told you I saw Monsieur Oh-So-Fashionable yesterday." He swirled the rum in his cup. "The Bourdon children were there with Blanchet, but I didn't see Marietta when I strode up and greeted him. Blanchet told me she was on the ice slide with Raoul. The man was talkative, I'll tell you that. He was keen to speak of things he shouldn't have been talking about, probably because he knew I would eventually tell everything to you."

"Tell me what?"

"Blanchet has bought a ring."

Philippe mouthed the word, his mind balking at the implications, thinking André must be talking of a signet ring or some other kind of ring on Blanchet's finger, for Blanchet was a man who took great care in his appearance—

"Courtships are short here," André warned. "You know this."

Philippe shook his head, addled, the lines of the riddle swimming in his mind, shifting, *without her presence there would be—of happiness—a dearth.*

"The ring," André continued, "is for Marietta. He showed it to me. Blanchet assured me, in no uncertain terms, that he plans to give the ring to her on New Year's Day. Probably at the réveillon."

Philippe's gaze shifted to the tavern keeper's prized possession, one of only five clocks in all of the Quebec settlement, brought over from Paris, hanging behind the wooden bar.

It was not yet midnight, New Year's Eve.

Moments away from New Year's Day.

"Drink your rum, or don't drink your rum, as you choose." André tapped a finger on the wax tablet. "But, if you are going to be a sober man tonight, then you'd best figure out that riddle fast. In Quebec, marriage won't wait."

Philippe's fur-lined cloak was a bulwark against the bitterly cold night as he trudged toward the upper town. A black sky and a half-moon cast the mountainside road in glittering shades of blue and white. The buildings that lined the road loomed inky, as did the seminaries and the bell towers and soaring steeples at the top. He strode from shadow to shadow, half in shame, avoiding splashes of golden light spilling out of the windows where the New Year's feasts were in full gaiety all through the town. The rhythmic clatter of percussion bones and the vibrato strings of violins carried through the air as he set his step toward the Bourdon house.

He knew he shouldn't be doing this, that he should accept any choice the woman he loved might make, that approaching her tonight wasn't the most honorable way to convince her, and perhaps the worst way to woo. But he was *propelled* to do this, as he had been since the very first moment he'd laid eyes upon Marietta, and reason and common sense and good behavior and better intentions crumbled under this need to be her partner in life.

Glimpsing movement in the night, he paused at the corner of a stone seminary under construction. He crouched in the shadows so he could watch, undetected, as a tall, elegant figure swinging a cane approached the Bourdon home.

Damn.

The figure was that of Louis-Jacques Blanchet, now knocking at the front door.

Panic flooded through him. He slapped a hand on a cold hard stone until the grit bit into his palm and the ice numbed his fingers. He couldn't let this engagement happen. Marietta didn't know what he had been planning these last few days. She would consider him, he *knew* she would, if she only knew the new plans he had in mind.

Damn, he needed more time.

He needed a Christmas miracle.

The door to the Bourdons' house opened, and the light that spilled out put Blanchet's figure in silhouette. Marietta's beau was welcomed in, and then the door was shut behind him, leaving Philippe crouching in the shadows and sudden silence. With a dangerous surge of determination, he bolted into the street, no longer caring if anyone glimpsed him moving so late in the evening, figuring that everyone in the Bourdon house was currently distracted by the new arrival and so he could do what he must. He wasn't sure what he was going to do—only that he would unlikely be welcome if he knocked at the front door, but there might be an opportunity through the back door to sneak in and waylay Marietta in the hall or the foyer, perhaps as she darted to the kitchen to deliver dirty dishes or pick up a platter of food, or made her way outside to the privy on the far side of the garden. He had no idea what he was going to say to her, how he would explain himself. Options raced through his mind as he turned the corner and, seeing a figure in the garden, stopped short.

He supposed the motionless figure, alone in an open space among a few gnarled, leafless fruit trees whose branches were sugared with snow, could be any woman, one of the other King's Daughters or a servant or Madame Bourdon, but he knew who she was instantly. Something about the tilt of her head, the slope of her clavicle…and the way the moonlight fell upon her bare shoulders and pale face.

For a moment, he was sucked into his dream, seeing a moonlit flower in the middle of the woods.

The memory bolstered his doggedness.

They were fated to be together.

The crunch of his boots in the new-fallen snow caught her attention. She turned her face away from the stars and toward him as he approached. Her lips parted in a silent gasp.

He meant to use words. Truly, he did. A thousand persuasive arguments rose to his lips, and he had every intention of cupping her face with his hands—his hands, which were now bare. Sometime between when he'd first glimpsed her and now, when he stood a breath away from her in the little clearing between the trees, he'd shed his gloves, intending only to cup her face so she would not turn away, so she would be compelled to listen to the words he intended to say to her, but when his lips parted to speak, he found himself lowering his head and pressing his mouth against her wet, slightly parted one.

Her lips gave beneath his. She tasted of sweet pastry and savory gravy, of wine and nutmeg, and her hair smelled of pine resin and yule-log smoke. A rush of pleasure pushed away the chill of the night, lifted a groan to his throat, and made his fingertips curl a little deeper into the pillow of her cheeks. He tilted his head to press the kiss more firmly, and her head tilted, as well, and he became aware that she too was using her mouth to search for a closer fit with his. He slid one hand deep into the softness of her hair as he drowned in the closeness of Marietta.

"Philippe."

The whisper of his name against his mouth lifted him from the delirium. He became aware of a vague double pressure on his chest, the flat of her hands urging distance.

He raised his head and gave them both some space to breathe, which they both did, puffing out clouds of condensation. She lowered her head so he couldn't see her gleaming eyes, only the narrow white part of her scalp and the way the moonlight streaked her black hair with shades of blue.

"Philippe," she repeated in a husky voice that made his blood surge, "you shouldn't be here."

I know.

"I can't stay." She pressed her fingers against her throat, and Philippe saw with a rush of relief that she wore no ring—not yet. "I…I…just came out for a breath of air."

"Stay."

"But…but they'll all be wondering where I've gone. They'll come looking—and you can't be here—"

"Don't marry him, Marietta."

She stilled, pale face rising. Surprise and panic animated those dark, dark eyes.

"Please." She squeezed her eyes shut and

shook her head. "I have to get back to the party."

A hundred thousand words rose to his throat. *Listen, listen. I'm not going west come the fall. I'm making other plans. I want to stay here in this settlement with you, use the wealth of furs I've moved to a warehouse not to pay for a voyage of exploration, but to build a home for you and me, if you'll have me as your husband, and build a business too, a warehouse of my own and an agency to help fur traders navigate the new regulations to come now that the king has taken over management of the trade and the settlement.* He meant to speak all those words aloud, but none of them fell from his lips. They were words of reason, but in this singular moment of singing connection—she'd *welcomed* his kiss, he'd felt that welcome to the marrow of his bones—he knew this woman needed more than rationality to persuade her to forgo what common sense was telling her was the surer prospect, the better man in Louis-Jacques.

So he took a gamble and blurted a different, more profound truth.

"I love you, Marietta."

The fingers she held against her throat splayed. Her brow rippled as she swayed on her feet. She searched his face in the moonlight, and he willed her to believe him, to see how desperately he'd been seeking her, for so long, and how much he wanted to hear her say the same words back to him.

But she did not speak.

Instead, she surged up on her toes and canted forward, aiming those lovely wet lips toward his. He captured them for a second time, felt the warm tremors of her eagerness, and did what he couldn't keep himself from doing: He pulled her bodily against him. He cursed the thick coat that prevented him from feeling every inch of her, but he took advantage of her lack of outerwear to slide his bare hands over her lovely body—for she'd come straight from her seat at the feast, with the perfume of pine and smoke in her hair, not stopping to don a hat or gloves or cloak—and so his fingers soaked in the feeling of her warm body under the silk dress and boned bodice swelling and deflating with every heaving breath, the slimness of her waist, the soft curve of her hips beneath the layers of petticoat. Crouching slightly, he slid his arms beneath her plump bottom and hauled her up against him, moving them both out of the moonlight, slowly twirling her out of the clearing, into the deeper, inkier shadows of the house eaves, where the overflowing woodpile would block the view of any intruder stepping out the kitchen door in search of her, as she pressed her face against his hair and made no protest.

Capturing her lips anew, he found himself fumbling to gather up her skirts, to get closer to her, to slide his bare hand beneath and feel her skin—that was all he wanted, truly, just to slide his bare skin over hers—he would ask for no more….but her low-throated whimper urged him on. The trailing ends of her ribbon garter slid through his fingers as he found the soft, trembling flesh of her upper thigh. Breaking the kiss, she pressed her head back against the wood of the house. Seeing the pulse fluttering in her throat, he laid his lips upon her neck as his hand explored higher. She gifted him, for his efforts, a startled, hungry moan.

A thought passed through his mind that he was stealing what he did not yet possess, and yet when he paused in his caresses, she lowered her head, frowned at him, and wriggled against his hand in a way that could not be mistaken. She wanted this. The thought sent his blood surging. He wanted her, in so many ways more than this, and had he not dreamed of her? Were they not fated to be together? Was he not meant to seek and find her, just as he'd found her moments ago, her pretty face turned up to the moonlight?

So he conceded to her silent but insistent wishes and moved his hand in ways to heighten her pleasure. Burying his face in her throat, he kissed her racing pulse and sucked her earlobe into his mouth and ran the edge of his teeth against her throat in gentle love bites, resisting the urge to take any more than what she was offering, though his body ached to join her, and his mind ran ahead to what pleasures they could share together, in a warm bed, with a roof over their heads, in a place of privacy without the danger of interruptions, if she would only put *his* ring on her finger and agree to be his wife. As these thoughts ran through him, she suddenly stiffened and muffled a cry, and he knew, with a new rush of triumph, that he'd brought her to the peak of bodily pleasure.

He held her close and watched her face as her head tilted against the wall behind her, her eyes closed and her long lashes curled against her cheeks, her mouth swollen and slightly parted, her breathing growing slow and deep.

He could spend the rest of his life gazing upon this woman, kissing the length of that throat, watching as she blinked her eyes open, as he waited for a smile of wicked pleasure to stretch the corners of her lips, as he somehow knew it would.

But that pleasure was stolen from him as the back door squealed on its leather hinges, and firelight spilled out into the night.

Marietta's eyes flew open when she heard the voice that emerged.

"Now where did that girl go?" Madame Bourdon stepped outside. Over the woodpile, Philippe could just glimpse the swaying decorative feather that rose from the top of the lady's coiffure. "She's not anywhere in the house, so she must be out here somewhere…"

Marietta, wide-eyed, wriggled against him. He let her go and shuffled back only enough so Marietta could find her feet, but not far enough to be visible within Madame Bourdon's line of vision.

Frustration coiled in his gut.

He'd run out of time

"Don't marry that man," he whispered, seizing her arms to recapture her attention. "Wait for me."

Madame Bourdon, in a soft, wavering voice, as if she'd heard something, said, "Marietta, are you out here?"

Marietta swallowed and looked all around, looked at nothing, her expression rippling with so many emotions, too many for him to read, but he thought he saw confusion and indecision and astonishment and maybe a little embarrassment at the intimacy they'd just shared.

Madame Bourdon's footfall scraped

through the new snow as the lady took a step deeper into the garden. "My dear, you're frightening me. I'm sure you're out here."

Philippe let go of Marietta's arm and nudged her chin up so she had no choice but to look into his eyes. "Trust me, all will be well." He pressed his forehead against hers. "Just don't agree to marry him."

She breathed, *"Philippe,"* as Madame Bourdon took another step into the garden, and they had no more time.

He released her chin so she could escape him and make her own choice. "Remember this: I love you."

"Love." The word tumbled, breathless, from her lips, followed by the strangest of strangled laughs. "I suppose that's the answer to all things."

Then she was gone in a rustle of skirts, shooting by him to stride toward Madame Bourdon, speaking apologies in a loud voice, once she'd cleared the shelter of the woodpile, about how she had felt so dizzy from the wine, and just had to come outside for a breath of air.

He felt dizzy too, as Marietta and Madame Bourdon returned to the house, shutting the door behind them. He ran through everything she'd said, groping for some surety, finding none. He couldn't be sure he'd convinced her. He'd had so little time, and he'd chosen to use it delightfully, but perhaps unwisely. He canted forward, pressing his forehead against the wall where Marietta had stood only a moment before, praying her cryptic last words meant that she didn't loved Blanchet.

Aching with the hope that her last words meant she loved *him*.

CHAPTER THIRTEEN

How did she ever get herself in such a situation?

"No, no, my dear Louis," Marietta said, avoiding his eye and ignoring his impatience as she threw out a hand, palm first, in the general direction of where her beau sat in one of the comfortable hearthside, hay-stuffed chairs in Madame Bourdon's parlor. "The children must open their New Year's presents first, or we'll never have a moment's peace. You and I, we'll exchange gifts later." Flushed with warmth that was not caused by the hearth fire, Marietta wiggled her way to the very edge of the chair so she could reach for another New Year's present, the top one on a tumbling pile. "This one is for Raoul," she exclaimed, meeting the excited gaze of the four-year-old as he leapt up from the floor and raced to seize it from her hands. "I wonder," she teased the boy, tapping the tip of his nose. "What could it possibly be?"

Leaning back, she clasped her hands in her lap, worrying her fingers in the folds of the one blue silk dress left from her days as a diplomatic daughter, the best dress she owned. Raoul ripped into the wrapping with abandon. She probably should have pulled out a present for Helene, instead, for Helene had a habit of painstakingly folding the paper back from the box beneath, saving the old newsprint from France to read later, and thus took a lot more time to examine both wrapping and the gift inside—a privilege of the middle child to monopolize attention whenever possible. But even as Raoul squealed as he pulled a painted spinning-top from the box, Marietta had to resist the urge to glance above the hearth to the clock standing on the mantel, wondering when Philippe would come, or if she had just imagined his implicit promise last night and the words he'd spoken with such conviction.

I love you, Marietta.

She worried her lower lip with her teeth, remembering how he'd kissed and touched her last night as the moonlight streamed over them. *That* wasn't love—it was something much more primitive—but she had a whole lot of feelings that went with it. Her feelings for Philippe felt illicit, dangerously exciting, for they were born not from a formal courting, but because of his persistence and wit and intelligence. Those feelings had grown so strong that they had led to her behavior last night, made her willing to do things better done between a husband and wife, just because her heart begged her to.

She slid a quick glance toward Louis-Jacques, who leaned back in the overstuffed chair twirling the head of the cane in his hand, frowning behind his other hand as he watched Raoul, with the help of some of his siblings, get the top spinning on a spot where the edge of the rug gave way to smooth floorboards.

She suppressed a frustrated sigh. Louis-

Jacques was a good man. Even now, he waited in patience, though she knew he had a gift for her, the kind of special gift that came in a small wooden box. She suspected he'd planned to propose to her last night at the feast, but she'd pled a headache after she'd come in from the garden and had gone directly to her room instead. Were he to present his gift to her now, with the whole Bourdon family gathered in this parlor, Madame and Monsieur and all the children, and Isabelle and Delphine and her beaux and Emelie and hers... They would certainly expect her to say yes to such a fine match. Until the moonlight interlude with Philippe last night, she'd talked herself into saying yes, knowing Louis-Jacques would be a fine match, a good provider, and a kind husband. And now, her doubts crowded in, and her heart balked, and guilt was a sour sauce over it all. Louis-Jacques deserved better, after all his kindnesses. If she rejected him in such a public way, she'd be fickle and cruel.

And yet...this was her future at stake.

A future that she'd crossed a sea for, to

ensure it would be hers to choose.

Goodness, her mind was swimming. Wasn't it silly to think any woman could make a wise decision after only a few days or a week's acquaintance, with a stranger? To pick among so many men before knowing, really, what kind of life they could offer or the true measure of the man?

"Marietta."

She started as a shadow fell over her. She glanced up to find Louis-Jacques looming beside her chair, standing between her and the fire, while he ran his fingers over his thin mustache as if composing a speech.

No no no, not yet—

A loud knock startled them all.

"My goodness." Madame Bourdon popped up from her chair. "Whoever could be visiting at this hour? So early on New Year's Day?"

Marietta gripped the arms of her chair and leaned forward to see around Louis-Jacques, so she could glimpse who would come through the door. The angle wasn't quite right, but she could hear. Philippe's resonant voice came from the foyer, and a relief unlike any she'd known flooded through her.

Philippe stepped into the crowded room, swept the parlor with his gaze, and bowed in a way that would have been worthy in a royal palace. Her breath caught at the sight of him, the neatly combed-back hair, the broad, endless shoulders under his finely tailored woolen coat, with its fine horn buttons. The wicked scar that zagged through the left side of his face stretched and whitened as he gifted the room a smile. Her heart blossomed at the sight of him, and a great peace came over her. How could she have considered marrying for any reason but love?

What a fool she'd been.

"Thank you for allowing me to join you all, Madame Bourdon." Philippe nodded as he acknowledged each person in the room with gravity and respect. "Monsieur Bourdon. Ladies. Monsieur Blanchet. Children." In the long, intentional pause that followed, Marietta felt her color rising. "And, of course, I offer my best wishes for the New Year, especially to our darling Miss Marietta."

She gathered her skirts as if to stand, but her knees wouldn't quite comply, so she just bowed her head instead.

"Monsieur Martineau," she murmured. "How lovely to see you."

"Perhaps not so lovely." He pulled a rueful face as his gaze slid briefly to their hostess. "Forgive my intrusion, for I know the hour is young, but I could not resist." He stepped deeper into the room, into a small space within the circle of adults seated around a cluster of children and a pile of discarded paper and tumbled boxes on the floor. "Blame my boldness on an excess of enthusiasm, for I couldn't wait another moment to call upon Miss Marietta."

Louis-Jacques cleared his throat. "Sir, I believe that is my sole prerogative—"

"Louis." Marietta hated how she sounded like a scold. But she did not want a repeat of the tension of the card party, when she feared these men might come to blows. She was thrilled Philippe had arrived, uninvited, for many reasons—not least of which was that she was running out of ways to delay Louis's inevitable proposal. She hoped Philippe had some kind of plan—a plan that didn't involve fisticuffs or a discussion of a choice of dueling weapons. "Indeed, Louis," she continued, not to placate her beau, but because she wanted to be kind. "You *have* earned your place in this house today. But in the spirit of the season—and Madame Bourdon must agree—we must welcome all guests with enthusiasm and Christian charity."

She didn't meet her beau's eye, but she felt his disapproval and frustration.

"Marietta is very kind, but Monsieur Blanchet speaks truth," Philippe countered in a strong voice as he bowed to Louis-Jacques. "Right now, wooing Marietta is indeed your sole prerogative. I don't disagree with your point."

Marietta forcibly closed her mouth. What was Philippe up to? Louis seemed just as surprised, for his foot scraped against the floorboard as he turned sharply toward his rival.

"However," Philippe added, raising his hand, "Monsieur Blanchet's prerogative to woo Miss Marietta will soon no longer be exclusive, since I have a solution to the riddle. The *correct* solution."

As a gasp went up among the children, Delphine's squeal cut through it all. Marietta tightened her grip on the chair.

She had given up that option as lost.

Had Philippe truly solved it?

If so, he would save her from a very distressing duty. For the moment Philippe had walked into this room—or maybe last night, if she were being truthful—she had decided she would *not* marry dear, kind Louis-Jacques, no matter how heartfelt and practical and tempting his proposal. Philippe was the husband for her—for better or for worse— and even if it meant Philippe would make her a winter widow, she was resolved to marry him…even if it meant putting off a good man who deserved better, arbitrarily tossing aside the rules she'd made for herself and for the suitors of Quebec and bruising her good character in the process.

She'd been making decisions until now based on the worst aspects of her past…making decisions on what she *feared*.

Now it was as clear to her as perhaps it was to wise, witty, intelligent Philippe.

Love was the thing that mattered.

"If you've solved the riddle," Louis-Jacques said in a voice edged with challenge, "then speak, Martineau."

"It's quite simple. You'll all be astounded." Philippe's smile stretched the scar on his face in a playfully wicked way as he laid his soft blue eyes upon her. "Marietta, would you speak the first verse to us all?"

Every eye in the room turned toward her. She swallowed and gathered her wits before raising her voice to speak the words she knew by heart. "*My first is seen in pillared halls, Where kings and princes dwell; 'Tis found in every woodland vale, In every sunny dell.*"

"That whole verse," Philippe explained as she finished, "refers to a single letter. The first letter…of a word."

"A letter?" Louis-Jacques planted his cane deeper into the carpet. "What letter? What nonsense is this?"

"Listen carefully at what I emphasize as I

repeat it." Philippe lifted his voice. "*My first is seen in pillared halls where kings and princes dwell; 'Tis found in every woodland vale, in every sunny dell.* Do you hear?"

The children looked at one another, eyes wide, and many hands clapped many gaping mouths.

"L!" Jean-Baptiste blurted out, jolting up from his squat among his siblings. "All those words have the letter 'L' in them."

Marietta's pressed a hand against her heart. Philippe was not bluffing. He'd figured it out, this man of contradictions. Love had not deceived her, but led her to a man with gritty determination and all the natural intelligence he needed to win that which he'd set his heart upon.

He loves me, truly.

Gathering her wits, she spoke the second verse aloud, adding her own emphasis. "*Upon the yellow sandy beach, The ocean billows roar, My next—you'll find it in the foam, Rippling upon the shore.*"

"Foam…shore," Louis-Jacques murmured, in a deflated voice. "The second letter of the answer is…O.”

At the sound of Louis-Jacque's deflated voice, dismay corkscrewed through her. Poor Louis, he deserved so much better.

“Correct, Monsieur Blanchet. The second letter is 'O.'” Philippe took a few steps deeper into the room, rounding the cluster of children on the floor to get closer to her. “Speak the next two verses, Miss Marietta. Now that the code is broken, perhaps the children can figure out the next two letters, to finish the word that is the solution to the puzzle.”

She obliged, speaking around a lump rising in her throat. *“within the dark and gloomy* **cave***, Hid from the sun's bright glare, Precious jewels line the walls, And my third is always there.”* The verse was trickier than the others. It was the verse that puzzled her and her father most, when her mother first offered the riddle up to them. Now, here in this room, this verse had the same effect, for frowns and squints and rippled brows abounded, except upon the sober face of Louis-Jacques, whose head bowed as if under the weight of the answer.

I'm so, so sorry, Louis.

But I must follow my heart.

She continued the recitation where she left off. "*My fourth and last is found in France, But never seen in Spain; It has always been in England's clime, In every monarch's reign.*"

"So, if you've been paying attention," Philippe said, "you should now have four letters that spell out, in order, the remarkably simple solution. The last verse doesn't offer up a letter, but instead explains the value and necessity of the answer."

Philippe nodded at her with a twinkle in his eye and she obliged by reciting the last four lines. "*My whole from Jupiter's court on high, Descends to cheer the earth; Without his presence there would be, of happiness, a dearth.*"

Philippe raised his brows at the children. "Do you all understand it now?"

Many shook their heads, two of the older ones nodded, grinning. In seats next to their beaus, Isabelle and Delphine looked baffled. Beside her, Louis-Jacques let out a sigh of defeat like a long, slow bellow.

"Say it," Louis-Jacques urged Philippe,

impatience in his voice. "Speak the solution and let us be done."

"As you wish." Philippe bowed his head toward his rival in a sign of respect that lifted Philippe another dozen notches in her esteem. "The answer to the puzzle is love…L-O-V-E, which is the answer to all things."

Her heart jumped and started again, racing faster than before, as Philippe repeated the words she'd spoken to him last night. So *that* was how he figured out the riddle. She had not meant it as a hint, but the words must have stuck with him as he tried to work the riddle out. She felt suddenly light-headed, a buzzing rising in her ears, as all around her, the children shouted and chattered and the adults turned to one another, working it all out among themselves.

"Love comes from above," Philippe continued, anchoring her with his intense blue gaze, "and it cheers the earth, and without it, there would be no happiness on earth. As I have discovered these past days, as I fell in love with our dear Marietta."

Suddenly, she was standing, swaying on

wobbly legs. A hand clamped around her arm, Louis-Jacques's grip holding her upright.

"Are you quite well, Miss Marietta?"

"Oh." *Still so kind, even after all this.* "I am, Louis. I'm just…surprised." She extracted herself from his grip with as much delicacy as she could muster and turned her attention to Philippe. "You've solved the riddle, Monsieur Martineau. 'Love' is the correct answer."

Applause all around, and shouts of delight. She wondered if actors upon the French stage ever felt unsettled at the sudden applause as she did at this moment, as if just realizing she was the center of all attention…and forgot what she was supposed to say.

What should she say?

"As per the rules I set up"—was she stumbling over her words or was that her imagination?—"you are welcome to court me, Monsieur Martineau, if that be your wish."

"I've wished for nothing as fervently as that." Philippe raised one finger. "With the exception of one thing."

After glancing pointedly at Louis-Jacques,

Philippe bent a leg and lowered himself before her. Discarded wrapping crackled as his knee hit the floor.

Louis-Jacques, standing beside her, made a strangled sound to match her own, but Marietta barely heard either above the buzzing in her ears.

"I've been told that courtships in Quebec are very short," Philippe said. "Let ours be the shortest. Will you marry me, Miss Marietta?"

Yes.

Yesyesyesyesyesyesyesyesyesssss.

The word danced on the tip of her tongue, but she put a rein on it, holding it back. Her silence spread and infected the room, making the air feel thick. Louis-Jacques stood beside her. She could feel his body's warmth, his taut expectation.

She could put off the inevitable no longer. Looking up at her first suitor, she found his attention fixed upon her, as if he were trying to bore through her skull to read her most secret thoughts.

She opened her mouth twice to speak, but didn't find the words until the third time. "My dear Louis—"

"Please." Louis-Jacques raised a hand, showed her his smooth palm, and sighed. "I know when I'm bested."

She wanted to deny it—bested was such a harsh word. She had not, in the end, set these two men side by side in her mind, ticking off good qualities and bad to see who won the comparison. Instead, she had let love choose—and yet she could think of no words that wouldn't cause a good man pain.

No words except "I'm so sor—"

"No apologies necessary." He flicked his fingers as if to wave her words away. "I am a man of the world, dear Marietta. I recognize an abiding affection when I see it. And I know better than to press my case for selfish reasons. It's futile to come between those who hold such strong mutual feelings."

She pressed her hand against her heart, swaying again at the depths of his understanding, all while wondering how she'd nearly given herself away.

Dear, dear Louis.

"I confess," Louis added, with a tilt of his

head and a smile that he must have forced, yet managed to make it not look so, "I had hoped you and I would make a partnership where strong feelings might blossom over time, but it seems fate has intervened in a most unexpected way."

Louis-Jacques's attention shifted to the side, to where Philippe remained on bended knee, a forearm resting across his thigh. From the corner of her eye, Marietta saw Philippe offer another respectful bow of his head.

"Now," Louis-Jacques said, stepping away from her as he straightened his coat and took in the rest of the room with a glance, "I think I should leave you all and make my obligatory New Year's Day visit to the governor, who is, after all, expecting me."

Exquisite grace, Marietta thought, and a perfect way to exit. Her father would have admired his diplomacy and intelligence.

"Miss Isabelle." Louis-Jacques spoke the name like a command, raising his chin in Isabelle's direction, to where she sat on the far side of the room. "Will you be so kind to help me fetch my hat, gloves, and coat? There is quite a pile of coats out there. I would be much obliged."

Isabelle's eyes widened at the request, and then the girl all but floated off her chair to make her way out of the parlor. Perhaps it was her imagination, but Marietta thought she glimpsed a shine in Isabelle's eyes. My goodness, had Isabelle been nurturing feelings for Louis? Marietta hadn't noticed that, but, then again, she'd been so distracted lately with her own affairs. Catching her breath, Marietta turned to Louis-Jacques, who now followed Isabelle's slim figure with his eyes before striding after her into the foyer.

Now *there* was a fine match, Marietta thought. Oh, wouldn't it be wonderful if Isabelle married Louis-Jacques? Now that Louis was free of the challenge that Marietta and that riddle had offered, Louis-Jacques just might be ready to recognize the hidden jewel that was Isabelle.

She caught her hands together and then turned to Philippe, still crouched on one knee before her, his lips stretched in a knowing smile.

She couldn't help but smile herself, and indulge in a bit of teasing.

"Monsieur Martineau." She straightened up. All the dizziness had fled. "What was that you were saying to me earlier?"

"I believe," he drawled, pushing off his thigh to straighten himself up, "you were about to say 'yes.'"

She widened her eyes in innocence. "Say yes to what, pray tell?"

Light laughter all around. Everyone else somehow knew her assent to marriage with Philippe was inevitable, a matter of easy humor, but a girl was only proposed to once, for a lifetime, if she were lucky, and she made it memorable.

"Say yes"—he grinned, rifling through his pockets—"to putting me out of my misery by becoming my wife."

She barely looked at the ring he offered, a blur of silver and sparkle, in favor of those laughing blue eyes.

"Monsieur Philippe…my answer is *yes.*"

CHAPTER FOURTEEN

With a stomach full of the richest food, Philippe pushed his chair a fraction back from Madame Bourdon's table. The room was full of people celebrating the double celebration: The traditional, lively, and often raucous feast of the three kings, as well as his swiftly arranged wedding to his breathtaking wife.

"Don't look at me with that gleam in your eyes," Marietta murmured, leaning into him. "I know what you want. But we can't sneak away until our hostess cuts the *galette de rois* and we discover who gets the piece with the pea in it. There's a prize, you know."

"I've got my prize already." Though it was

the first week of January, Marietta smelled of cherry blossoms, some perfume or soap she'd used as she'd prepared for their wedding, and all he wanted to do was bury his face in her neck and naked bosom and wherever else was necessary in order to find the source of that scent on her warm, naked skin. "Just tell them you're off to the privy and—"

"Don't be silly. They'll wait for us to return. We're the guests of honor, remember?"

She touched her nose to his, then, leaning back, she ran a finger down his scar. Just yesterday, he'd told her all about how he got that scar, and promised, as he did, they would never have secrets between them.

"After the galette. Then we'll go." She sucked in one plump lip and then dug her teeth gently into it. He loved when she did that. "And then," she added, her voice dropping, husky, "maybe we can finish what you started last week in the shadow of that woodpile."

"No."

She reeled back, surprised. He enjoyed the

view of her breasts swelling above the low cut of her gown, the way the firelight caught upon the pale ribbons in her hair, and how wet and inviting her lips were, parted like that in surprise.

"Not the woodpile. We need a bed this time." He took her hand and raised it to his lips. "We'll need plenty of room to move about."

Even in the dim light, he could see the color rise to her cheeks. Yet it wasn't shyness he saw. She radiated encouragement, laughter, and excitement, an eager willingness to explore. Fortunately, his wedding coat fell to midthigh, so when he eventually stood, no one would be able to see the extent of his excitement, except perhaps his wife. He knew he was a lucky man already, but he suspected he didn't know the full extent of his luck, not yet.

He squeezed her hand and turned back to the revelry to distract himself and try to tame his raging urges. A violinist tuned his instrument in a corner, and a percussionist rattled a rhythm with bones in the opposite corner. Madame Bourdon stood up, wielding a knife, and began cutting the cake and sliding pieces upon pewter plates to be randomly passed around the party. A servant slid a plate before him, but he ignored it. It smelled delicious, but not as good as his wife, so he bided his time as the guests dug in, until a little while later, the arm of Jean-Baptiste shot up as he claimed the pea found in his cake.

The gift given—a fine painted wooden chess set—the musicians took their cue to stand and gather at the far end of the room to begin the music. The guests rose from the table as if in unison to push the chairs to the walls and nudge the trestle table to make a space for dancing. He took advantage of the noise and music to urge Marietta up and head around the far end of the table, his wife in tow. Philippe tried to avoid every eye, but many guests seemed complicit in his effort to hurry the wedding night, only smiling and dropping their gazes as he tugged Marietta into the hallway, and deeper into the dimness.

He wove through the kitchen and the giddy, weaving servants, before bursting out into a cold he barely felt above the heat of his excitement.

Marietta was all rollicking laughter, her hair bouncing upon her bare shoulders, her skirts flying with the speed of their flight. In the middle of the garden—starlit this time, as the moon had waned—he pulled her into his arms, and with her soft curves pressed against him, he laid a kiss upon those lips until the laughter retreated into her throat and shifted to moans.

"Marietta. My darling Etta." He couldn't get enough of her. He planted kisses on her lips and eyelids and earlobe and throat and dug his fingers under the edge of her bodice, wanting so much to yank it down, but not here, not now. "I've rented a house for us"— what an inelegant fool he was, blurting this out. It was supposed to be a surprise, a wedding gift, a place of their own in which to start their married life—"It's only two doors down."

"I know."

He raised his head. He'd told no one about the home but André, who'd been tasked with lighting a fire in every hearth before he and Etta arrived, which his old friend better be doing, right this moment.

"I also know about your new plans," she added. "How you want to build a warehouse in the lower town, and be an agent for André's voyage—"

"Monsieur Bourdon must have told you," he interrupted, a little annoyed. He'd hope to tell her all about it himself. "I expected him to have more discretion."

"My darling husband." She shook her head and patted his cheek. "Don't blame my host. He didn't say a word, but the door of his office is thin, and I have overheard many things."

"Eavesdropping?"

"Not intentionally."

She shrugged, and for a moment, he was distracted by the rise of her pale shoulder, and how the motion revealed another inch of fleshy breast above the neckline of her bodice, and his mouth began to water.

"As for the location of our wedding night," she continued, "I heard about that from Madame Bourdon. I asked her this morning if she intended to put a room aside for us, for our wedding night—for you hadn't said a word about that—and she said you'd made 'arrangements' at old Monsieur Bois's home."

"This was the last secret I intended to keep, I promise."

"You broke no promise," she said. "You meant it as a surprise, a gift, and I adore surprise gifts."

She pressed against him in a way that added new tension in his breeches. He cupped her face, pale in the starlight, her eyes deep pools of love.

For a moment, he thought about his dream of the stag and the moonlit flower. Only now did he realize he hadn't had the dream since she'd agreed to marry him.

Of course he hadn't.

He no longer needed the dream.

He'd finally found the one precious gift he'd been looking for.

THE END

Author's Note

Book lovers who've already read the other novels in the King's Girls Series will recognize Marietta and Philippe as important secondary characters in the series. I've longed to write their love story, but didn't quite know how to frame it until my muse offered up the idea of using a riddle.

In olden tales, riddles were sometimes used as a way for a woman to filter marriage prospects. So, when I happened to stumble upon a 17th century book of English riddles, I figured it was the hand of fate…and so *A Husband By Christmas* was born.

For the sake of historical accuracy, I shared the long riddle in this story from "Merry's Book of Puzzles" by J. N. Sterns. I bow with profound thanks to Project Gutenberg for providing unrestricted use of this centuries-old-out-of-print book for the general public.

Don't miss the other novels in the King's Girls Series

HEAVEN IN HIS ARMS: Book One

Struggling to survive on the streets of Paris, Genny agrees to a dangerous masquerade: She switches places with a King's Girl, a young noblewoman about to be shipped to the colonies. It's a risky venture with a high price—once overseas, Genny must marry a stranger....

THE WINTER HUSBAND: Book Two

Jailed for crimes unbecoming a lady, Marie yearns for liberty even as she refuses the one choice that will set her free: An arranged marriage with a frontier stranger. Then a brawny ex-soldier offers a more dangerous proposal. Spend one winter as his wife in name only, and come spring he will set her free…

ABOUT THE AUTHOR

Lisa Ann Verge is a critically acclaimed RITA© nominated author whose dozens of novels have been published worldwide and translated into seventeen languages.

She started her career writing emotionally intense romance about sexy men and dangerous women, and now as **Lisa Verge Higgins** she also writes life-affirming women's fiction.

A finalist for RT Book awards five times over, Lisa has won the Golden Leaf and the Bean Pot, and twice she has cracked Barnes & Noble's General Fiction Forum's top twenty books of the year.

When not writing, she can be found hunting wild mushrooms, learning Turkish, and keeping track of her three adult daughters, whose adventures make life interesting.